D0267702

SIEGFRIED

ALSO BY HARRY MULISCH

The Assault
Last Call
The Discovery of Heaven
The Procedure

HARRY MULISCH
SIEGFRIED

TRANSLATED BY PAUL VINCENT

VIKING
an imprint of
PENGUIN BOOKS

VIKING

Published by the Penguin Group
Penguin Books Ltd, 80 Strand, London WC2R 0RL, England
Penguin Putnam Inc., 375 Hudson Street, New York, New York 10014, USA
Penguin Books Australia Ltd, 250 Camberwell Road, Camberwell, Victoria 3124, Australia
Penguin Books Canada Ltd, 10 Alcorn Avenue, Toronto, Ontario, Canada M4V 3B2
Penguin Books India (P) Ltd, 11 Community Centre, Panchsheel Park, New Delhi - 110 017, India
Penguin Books (NZ) Ltd, Cnr Rosedale and Airborne Roads, Albany, Auckland, New Zealand
Penguin Books (South Africa) (Pty) Ltd, 24 Sturdee Avenue, Rosebank 2196, South Africa

Penguin Books Ltd, Registered Offices: 80 Strand, London WC2R 0RL, England

www.penguin.com

Originally published in Dutch as *Siegfried* by Uitgeverij de Bezige Bij, Amsterdam 2001
Published in the United States of America by Viking Penguin 2003
Published in Great Britain by Viking 2003
1

Copyright © Harry Mulisch, 2001
Translation copyright © Paul Vincent, 2003

The moral rights of the author and translator have been asserted

Printed in Great Britain by Clays Ltd, St Ives plc

A CIP catalogue record for this book is available from the British Library

ISBN 0-670-91271-9

Why doesn't the devil carry me off?
It must be better with him than here.

EVA BRAUN,
Journal, March 2, 1935

SIEGFRIED

ONE

As the landing gear hit the concrete with a thump, Rudolf
Herter started awake from a deep, dreamless sleep. The aircraft braked with a roar of its engines and turned off the runway in a smooth arc. *Flughafen Wien.* He sat up with a slight
groan; he had taken off his shoes and was massaging the toes of
his left foot with a pained expression.

"What's wrong?" asked the tall, much younger woman sitting next to him. She had red hair that she wore up.

"I've got a cramp in my index toe."

"In your what?"

"In my index toe." He smiled and looked into her big, green
and brown eyes. "It's funny how every bit of your body has a
name—nostril, ear, elbow, palm—except for the two toes to
the left and right of your middle toe. They've been forgotten."
He laughed and said, "I hereby dub them the index toe and the
ring toe. Behold the completer of the work of Adam, who gave
things their names." He looked at her. "For that matter, Maria
isn't all that far away from Eve."

"I see you're your usual idiotic self," said Maria.

1

"It's my job."

"Had a pleasant trip, Mr. Herter?" asked the steward, bringing their coats.

"Apart from drinking a quarter bottle too much of Alsace wine over Frankfurt. Terrible. These days every glass of wine costs me ten minutes' extra sleep."

Because they were traveling business class, they were able to leave the aircraft first. Herter looked into the happy, wide-eyed faces of the assembled crew; the captain had also appeared in the doorway of the cockpit.

"Good-bye, Mr. Herter. Enjoy your stay in Vienna," he said with a broad smile, "and thanks for your wonderful book."

"I was only doing my duty," said Herter with a grin.

In the baggage-claim area, Maria tugged a trolley from the telescoped row, while Herter leaned against a pillar with his coat over his arm. The abundant hair around his sharply etched face sprang like flames from his head but at the same time was as white as the foam on the surf. He wore a greenish tweed suit with a vest, the function of which seemed to be to hold his tall, narrow, fragile, almost transparent frame together; after two cancer operations and a brain hemorrhage, he felt physically a shadow of the shadow of his former self—but only physically. He turned his cool, gray-blue eyes on Maria, who, like a hound at a foxhole, kept her eyes riveted on the rubber flaps, which one moment let through a calfskin Hermès bag, the next a shabby package tied with string. She, too, was slightly built, but thirty years younger and thirty times stronger than he was. With powerful swings she pulled each of their suitcases off the conveyor belt and put it on the trolley in a single movement.

As they came through the sliding doors into the arrivals terminal, they were confronted by a long line of signs and pieces of paper being held aloft: HILTON SHUTTLE, DR. OBERKOFLER, IBM, FRAU MARIANNE GRUBER, PHILATELIE 1999 . . .

"No one for us," said Herter. "I'm always shoved into the corner and sneered at by everyone." He felt giddy.

"Mr. Herter!" A small, beaming, obviously pregnant lady headed straight toward him and put out her hand. "I recognize you, of course, like everyone else. Thérèse Röell from the Dutch embassy. I'm the ambassador's right-hand man."

Herter leaned forward, smiled, and kissed her hand. A heavily pregnant right-hand man. This was the sort of thing he liked so much about Holland: the good humor. At those countless literary-political conferences that he had attended in his lifetime (all equally useless, by the way), the atmosphere was always liveliest among the Dutch delegations. While the Germans and French gathered in ponderous seriousness to work out their strategy for the following day, the Dutch invariably formed an exuberant group. Even in the cabinet, he had been told by a ministerial friend, they were regularly doubled up with laughter.

The embassy car was waiting right outside the exit; the chauffeur, a man with a huge handlebar mustache, held the doors open. It suddenly felt much colder than in Amsterdam. In the backseat Herter discussed his program with the right-hand man. Maria, whom he had introduced as his companion, sat in front next to the driver, but was half turned toward them so that she could follow the conversation—not only out of interest but also because she knew that he would find it even more difficult than usual to understand what was said, as his hearing aid also amplified the sound of the engine. Now and then he glanced at her, whereupon she repeated Mrs. Röell's words more or less unobtrusively. In order to conserve energy, the organizers had been very selective. Today there was just a short television interview for a cultural-affairs program, which would be broadcast later in the evening, giving him sufficient time to unpack and freshen up. Tomorrow morning there were interviews with three leading dailies and weeklies, lunch with the ambassador, and then, in the evening, the reading. He would have Thursday completely to himself. Mrs. Röell handed over the documentation and some newspapers with preliminary pieces on his work, which he immediately passed on to Maria. He made a brief movement with his eyebrows, so that Maria knew she had to take over the conversation at this point.

The city received them into the magnificent, monumental embrace of the Ringstrasse. He did not often visit Vienna, but each time he did, he felt more at home here than in any other city. His family came from Austria; obviously people carried in their genes the imprint of towns and landscapes where they themselves had never been. It was busy, the low November sun making everything vivid and precise; the last autumn leaves on the trees were few enough to count, and after the next storm they, too, would be gone. As they drove past a bright green park, covered with golden yellow leaves, Herter pointed to them and said, "That's how I often feel these days."

At the majestic Opera House, the car made a right turn and stopped at the Hotel Sacher. Mrs. Röell apologized for not being able to attend the lunch or reading tomorrow but said she would collect them on Thursday evening and take them to the airport.

At the reception desk in the busy lobby, he was welcomed

with delighted surprise, like someone for whom the luxurious hotel had been waiting for years. Herter took the whole thing in good spirits, but since he had never seen himself the way others had seen him for decades, he thought, All this is intended for an eighteen-year-old lad just after the Second World War, desperately poor and unknown, who is trying to get a story down on paper. But perhaps, he thought with amusement as the porter followed with their suitcases down long corridors carpeted and furnished in red, with nineteenth-century portraits in heavy gilt frames, the reality was less modest—perhaps it was completely the other way around: he was indeed unchanged, in the sense that for himself he had always been as he now was for others, too, even in his attic with the frost flowers on the windows.

On the table in the lounge of the spacious suite, a corner room that, with its crystal chandeliers and romantic paintings, looked like a boudoir of the Empress Sissi, stood a vase of flowers, a large dish of fruit with two plates, cutlery and napkins, and a bottle of sparkling wine in a silver-plated cooler. Next to two small traditional Sachertorten, Viennese chocolate cakes, lay a handwritten welcome note from the manager. After the operation of all the necessary buttons had been explained to them, Herter immediately started unpacking in order to remove the traces of the journey and to begin the next phase. Meanwhile, sitting on the edge of the bed, Maria phoned his estranged wife, Olga, to report their safe arrival; Olga was the mother of his grown-up daughters; in Amsterdam she was now looking after Marnix, the seven-year-old son of Maria and Herter. While Maria ran the bath and undressed, Herter went over to the corner windows.

Across the street the eye saw only the side wall of the imposing, Renaissance-style Opera House; in the square next to the hotel, by the mounted statue on its pedestal, stood a row of horse-drawn cabs for the tourists, the horses with blankets over their backs, the coachmen and coachwomen in long coats and capes and bowler hats. A little farther on was the Albertina Museum and behind it the towers and domes of the Hofburg could be seen in the thin autumn air.

Herter's thoughts went back to his first visit to Vienna forty-six years ago. He was twenty-six, bursting with vitality, and a year previously had published his first novel, *The Scarecrow*, which was awarded a prize while still in manuscript. When, at the age of fifty, he won the National Prize for Literature, the government representative called him a "born National Prize–winner," and he felt the same way. These kinds of things were part and parcel of his life, but back in 1952 no one except himself knew that yet. A journalist friend had to do an international report for an illustrated weekly and asked if he would come along. There were virtually no autobahns then, and they drove to Vienna in a Volkswagen along provincial roads via Cologne, Stuttgart, and Ulm. At that time, halfway through the twentieth century, the Second World War was only just over; cities lay in ruins, and the pair of them slept in the underground shelters that had been turned into temporary hotels. Vienna was also still full of rubble. Two memories had remained with him most vividly. The first was waking up the morning after his arrival in his shabby hotel in the Wiedner Hauptstrasse, not far from here. His room looked out onto a courtyard, and when he opened the window, he was struck by a completely new sensation: he could smell a vague, sweet smell, which he remembered without ever having smelled it before. Could one inherit the memory of smells? What's more, there was no temperature. The still air was not a fraction cooler or warmer than his skin; it was as if he were merging with the world. In some way he felt as if he had come home to his father, with whom by that time any further communication was impossible. The second memory was a meeting a few days later. Vienna was still occupied by the four Allies; on the façade of the Hofburg, where in 1938 Hitler had been acclaimed, now hung a gigantic Soviet star with the hammer and sickle. Exactly how this meeting had come about he could no longer remember, but there, in the Russian sector, he had got to talking with a soldier from the Red Army: a few years younger than he, a head shorter, garrison cap perched at an angle on his dark blond hair, supple boots and belt around his wide, overhanging peasant tunic with its epaulets. "Got to talking" was not quite the right description, since neither could understand a word of what the other was saying, and all Herter learned was that the soldier's name was Yuri and that he had come here from the vast depths of the Soviet Union to make sure that Hitler's seed did not germinate again. For several hours they walked through Vienna with their arms around each other's waists, pointing out the Austrians to each other and repeating a single text:

"*Germanski niks Kultur.*"

Where was Yuri now? If he were still alive, he would be approaching seventy. Herter sighed deeply. Perhaps he should write it all down at some point. It would be time for his memoirs by now, if it were not that his whole work consisted of memoirs: not only of his actual life but also of his imagination—the two being inseparable. There was a knock at the door; a porter set down a large bouquet, from the ambassador.

Herter looked back down at the square. The coachmen in

their monkey suits were tending their horses, and from behind a balustrade the bronze duke on his bronze horse also surveyed the city. In an empty part of the square stood a large, modern monument, on the spot where hundreds of Viennese had died during a bombing raid. That, too, they owed to their prodigal son, whom they had embraced adoringly a few years before on the Heldenplatz.

TWO

The interviewer, Sabine, telephoned the room to say that she was waiting for him downstairs. Accompanied by Maria, he took the elevator down to the luxurious, mahogany-paneled lounge. All the armchairs and couches, set amid large mirrors and vases filled with huge bouquets, were occupied. He recognized Sabine by the German edition of his latest novel that she was carrying under her arm, like a signal used on a blind date. She also stood out among the bourgeois public with her jeans and man's white shirt (buttoned left over right instead of the other way around). Before joining her, he gave Maria a kiss on the forehead; it was her first time in Vienna, and she was going into town.

"See you later. We might as well eat here tonight."

"Do you need anything?"

"I've got everything."

He introduced himself to the young blond woman and asked her how long the interview would last. No more than five minutes or so. In her blue eyes there was the usual shining look of admiration that he knew so well and that still embarrassed him. She looked at him, but in a strange, dual way: on the one hand as someone normally looks at a person, on the other the way someone looks at a thing, a work of art. What good to him was that admiration, which at the same time created a distance? All his life he had simply done as he pleased, since otherwise he would have been bored to death, and, as a result, he himself had turned increasingly into a work of art. What had he actually accomplished to deserve it? Of course, most people were incapable of writing good books, but he could not understand that inability any more than he could his own talent. It was obvious that he was able to write good books. To understand their incomprehension, he had to think of a composer or a painter: how the hell could one ever create a symphony or a painting? Bach and Rembrandt in turn would not understand his incomprehension. You simply had to *do* it. The fact that those deeds then led to magnificent temples of music, opera houses, derivative phenomena such as conductors, musicians, museums, theaters, libraries, statues, scholarly books, street names, and a look like the one in Sabine's eyes was nothing short of a miracle.

In a side room, its walls covered from top to bottom with signed photos of famous and forgotten guests, none probably still alive, everything was in readiness for the taping. He shook hands with the cameraman, the sound engineer, and the lighting technician, each of whom made a small bow, which no one in Holland would ever dream of doing. In a red-plush armchair, he crossed his legs, the lens and the lights focused on him, the boom above his head with the microphone on it like the fluffy cocoon of a huge insect, Sabine right next to the camera in an upright chair.

"One, two, three, four," she said.

The sound man turned a knob and looked at him.

"'All things corruptible, are but a parable,'" said Herter. "'Earth's insufficiency here finds fulfillment; here the ineffable wins love through love. . . .'"

Sabine looked up from her notes with a smile and said, "'Eternal Womanhood leads us above.'"

The sound man, who had probably not even realized that the climax of *Faust* was being quoted but had simply adjusted the volume, nodded. "Running."

"Running."

Although he had been in front of the camera hundreds of times, for almost as long as television had existed, he was still invariably overcome by a mild excitement when it came to the point. It had nothing to do with stage fright, because he knew he would get by easily, but more with the alienating effect of the situation: he looked into Sabine's eyes and then into the all-seeing third eye, glassy and pale as that of a dead fish, which would ensure that this evening would be a conversation watched by hundreds of thousands of eyes, now all focused on something different.

"Welcome to Vienna, Rudolf Herter from Amsterdam. To-morrow evening in the National Library, you will be reading from your magnum opus, *The Invention of Love*, which has found countless enthusiastic readers in Austria as elsewhere. It is a modern version of the medieval legend of Tristan and Isolde, a moving novel of almost a thousand pages, though for many people that is still too few. Can you give viewers a brief notion of your book?"

"No, I can't, and I'll tell you why." He was of course an old hand; the question had been put to him scores of times, and he knew exactly what he was going to say. That the subject itself didn't matter that much. That one could, for example, decide to write a play about a young man whose father had been murdered by his uncle, who then went on to marry his mother, whereupon he resolved to avenge his father but did not manage it. That could result in a melodrama that no one wanted to see, but if one were called Shakespeare, the result was *Hamlet*. That what mattered in art was always the *how*, never the *what*. That in art the form was the real content. That his own book was indeed a variation on the theme of Tristan and Isolde, but that could equally well have resulted in a cloyingly sentimental novel.

"Which is not the case," said Sabine. "On the contrary, it is the compelling story of two people who are not soul mates but through a fatal misunderstanding—which I won't give away—conceive a passionate love for each other. They deceive each other, are constantly driven apart, but are still reunited until, again as a result of lies and deceit, they finally die their harrowing lovers' death."

"Goodness me," said Herter with a smile. "Now *you've* given viewers a notion of my book." His German was a little old-fashioned, from before the First World War, but virtually without accent.

"Of course you are right. This in itself means nothing. What matters is the fantastic fantasy with which it is written. Can I put it like that?"

"You can put it any way you like. 'Fantastic fantasy' . . . to tell you the truth, I always have a bit of a problem with the term 'fantasy.' It smacks of something active, like a water-skier behind a roaring speedboat, where a better image would be a surfer riding the ocean passively and silently and letting himself be carried along by the waves."

"What should I call it then? Imagination?"

"Let's go on calling it fantasy."

"I'd like to talk to you a little more about that. Is creative fantasy like dreaming?"

"Not only that. It is also a way of understanding. In that, I appear to be following in the footsteps of your venerable fellow townsman Sigmund Freud, but that is not so. For him dreams, daydreams, myths, novels, and everything related to them were objects on which the understanding focuses, but what I mean is that they *themselves* are the understanding."

"I'm afraid I can't quite follow you."

"It's a problem for me, too, but I'll do my best. I mean that some types of artistic fantasy are not so much something that must be understood but rather something *with which* you understand. Fantasy of this kind is a tool. I'll try to turn everything around. Turning things around is always fruitful. Let me give you an example. . . ."

"Please do."

With half-closed eyes, Herter nodded briefly and said, "Take a realistically painted theatrical set, as you occasionally see at the opera. For example, the sea, a fishing village, the dunes. That is extended onto the stage with an assortment of real objects, such as sand, fishing nets, rusty buckets. And what do you see? The painted backdrop seems like reality, but under artificial lighting and in the still air of the theater, all those real objects have taken on an unreal, artistic appearance. Am I making myself clear?"

"To tell the truth . . ."

"Right. Let me approach it differently." Herter thought for a moment, feeling that he was on the track of something. "Take someone who actually exists but whom you don't understand completely or don't understand at all."

"Rudolf Herter," said Sabine with an acute smile.

"That would be someone else's job," said Herter, also smiling. "Yours, for example. No, I don't mean a man whose words you can't understand, but a man whose *nature* you can't fathom. Or a woman, of course. Suppose I know a woman who is a mystery to me—"

"Do you know a woman like that?" asked Sabine, interrupting.

"Yes," said Herter, thinking of the mother of his daughters. The idea began to take shape in his head like a gathering storm. "If I'm correct in my view of fantasy, it must be possible to understand her better by placing her in a completely fictional, extreme situation and seeing how she behaves. By way of an intellectual—no, imaginative—experiment."

"I'm glad I'm not that woman," said Sabine with a hint of horror in her voice. "I don't know . . . experimenting with people . . . it sounds horrific to me."

Herter raised his arms. She now obviously regarded him as a kind of literary Dr. Mengele, but he was careful not mention that name.

"You're right! Perhaps it is not without danger to do such things with a living person whom you care for. Perhaps you can do it only with a dead person whom you hate."

"And do you know someone like that?"

"Hitler," said Herter at once. "Hitler, of course. I mean, I *don't* know him at all. Another fellow townsman of yours, by the way."

"Of whom we prefer not to be reminded," added Sabine.

"But it will continue for centuries. By now a hundred thousand studies have been devoted to him, if not more: political, historical, economic, psychological, sociological, theological, occult, and so on ad infinitum. He's been examined from all sides, a line of books has been written about him that would reach from here to the Stefansdom, more than about anyone else, but it hasn't gotten us anywhere. I haven't read everything—one lifetime is too short for that—but if anyone had explained him satisfactorily, I would know. He has remained the enigma that he was to everyone from the very beginning—or no, he has simply become more incomprehensible. All those so-called explanations have simply made him more invisible. If you ask me, he's sitting in hell laughing himself silly. It's time that was changed. Perhaps fiction is the net that he can be caught in."

"So a historical novel, in fact."

"No, no, that is a well-behaved genre that takes historical fact as its starting point and then tries to put, more or less plausibly, flesh and blood on the bare bones. Your fellow townsman Stefan Zweig was a master of that. Sometimes things become very intense, as in all those books and films reconstructing the assassination of President Kennedy, but the point I am getting at is the understanding of an event, not of a human being. A rabid moralist like the German dramatist Rolf Hochhuth starts with a fact from social reality, as in *The Representative*, about the fateful role of the pope in the Holocaust, and then lets his imagination loose on it; but I am thinking more of doing it the other way around. I want to start from some imagined, highly improbable, highly fantastic but not impossible fact and move from mental reality into social reality. That is, I think, the way of true art: not from the bottom up but from the top down."

"Hasn't that, too, already been done countless times with Hitler?"

"No doubt. But not yet by me."

"Well, we look forward to your story with curiosity. I'm sure you'll be able to bring it off."

"If the gods are well disposed, yes."

"Do you believe in God?"

"God is a story, too, but I am a polytheist, a heathen; I don't believe in one story, I believe in many stories. Not only Hebrew ones but also Egyptian and Greek. I myself have also—if I may be so bold—written more than one story."

"And are you working on a new story at the moment?"

"Always."

"How far have you gotten?"

"About a tenth of the way through, I estimate. You never know exactly beforehand, and that's just as well. If I had known that *The Invention of Love* would run to almost a thousand pages, I would never have begun it."

"Can you give us a sneak preview of your new novel?"

"Yes, but I'm not going to."

"Mr. Herter, I wish you every success for tomorrow, and thank you for the glimpse behind the scenes you have given us."

"On the contrary. I thank *you*. You have given me an idea."

THREE

"You're very quiet tonight," said Maria as they stood in the elevator after dinner, coffee, and chocolate. "Is something the matter?"

"Yes, something's the matter."

He gave her a dark look, and he saw that she realized it was something to do with his work and therefore did not question him further. They had drunk a bottle of wine each, too much in fact, but too much wine in Vienna is different from too much wine in Amsterdam. In his literary laboratory, he was constantly searching for an imagined experimental setup in which he could place Hitler in order to lay bare his underlying structure, and it disturbed him that he did not immediately know how to go about it. He took his mechanical pencil from his pocket and put the manager's welcome note on his lap. Beneath the logo of the hotel, which was stamped into the thick paper, an *S* in a laurel wreath surmounted by a crown, he wrote in block capitals:

ADOLF HITLER

He stared pensively at the words, but without reading them—he looked at the eleven letters as if at a drawing, an icon: the severe composition of horizontals and verticals, with the graceful concluding sweep.

I, DART OF HELL

HALF RIOT-LED

He looked at his watch, turned on the television in the sitting room, and found the channel.

"In five minutes I'm going to tell you on-screen what the matter is."

Seated side by side on the sofa, Herter and Maria watched the end of a report on an exhibition of Dürer: watercolors of birds' feathers in brilliant hues. He absorbed it intensely; whenever he was working on something, everything he saw and experienced was tested against the criterion of whether he could use it and fit it in. He suddenly remembered the gray pigeon's wing with which he used to brush the remnants of rubber off the sketchpad in drawing class—had Dürer used *his* pigeon wings for the same purpose? Wings, flying, flying away, freedom, Daedalus, Icarus . . . but cut off, torn out . . . No, the link between Dürer and Hitler had already been made by Thomas Mann in his *Doctor Faustus*, and he must keep away from that.

Titles, music: something from a Schubert piano sonata. A moment later he was looking at himself: but the man there on the screen was looking not at him but at someone next to him, in the place where Maria was now sitting.

"*Welcome to Vienna, Rudolf Herter . . .*"

He stretched his legs, put his hands, with fingers inter-twined, behind his head, and listened to his argument about the *what* and the *how* in art. Of course, he should have said that in music, the highest of the arts, no *what* even exists, only a *how*. When he said that imagination was not like a water-skier but like a surfer, he remembered an old observation that he had always wanted to find a home for but that he had still not been able to fit in anywhere: that technical development after the war had changed the silence of the beach into a constant din of speedboats and portable radios. But that with the further de-velopment of technology, prewar silence had returned: new materials had made windsurfing possible, which meant the end of waterskiing, and Walkmans were ousting radios.

He could be seen in thousands of Austrian homes; his voice was echoing through all those rooms, although he was now sit-ting here silently on the sofa. All quite normal—no one was as-tonished by it any longer—but at the same time it was an impossible miracle. He had preserved that astonishment from his childhood; and when he thought of himself, he did not think of a man of over seventy but of a child.

"Suppose I know a woman who's a mystery to me . . ."

"Do you know a woman like that?"

"Yes."

"I mean Olga," said Herter.

"Is that a fact?" asked Maria with an ironic smile.

Imagination as the tool of understanding. Without Sabine he would never have had the idea.

"Hitler. Hitler, of course."

When the interview was over, he turned off the sound and asked, "Do you understand?"

"Yes. But only because I know you."

"We might as well drink another glass to our meeting, then."

As the bottle of sparkling wine was now standing uselessly in water, he called room service for a bucket of ice.

"There's something I *don't* understand," said Maria. "Why Hitler, of all people? You want to place him in an extreme, fictional situation, but how can you dream up a more extreme situation for him than the one he dreamed up and realized himself? Why don't you take someone more moderate that you don't understand? There must be someone like that."

"He'd like that. Then he'll have been let off the hook yet *again*. No, it has to be Hitler. It has to be the most extreme figure in world history." Herter lit up a pipe and patted down the tobacco with his index finger for a moment. "But of course you're right; that's exactly the problem. That's what I've been walking around thinking about. Up to now I haven't gotten beyond one scene. We know that he never visited a concentration camp, let alone an extermination camp. He left that to Himmler, the head of the SS, and the police. Let's assume that one day he decided to go to Auschwitz to take a look at the daily gassing of thousands of men, women, and children, which he had ordered. How would he have reacted to that sight? But for that I must change his character, since that is precisely what he never did, and then I would have failed to understand him yet again."

"Was he too much of a coward?"

"Coward . . . coward . . . it's not as easy as that, of course. In the First World War, he was awarded the Iron Cross First Class for bravery as an orderly—very unusual for a corporal— and he always wore it. It was pinned on him by a Jewish officer, by the way. So he must have been exceptionally brave, but as far as I know, he never revealed what he won it for. I suspect he wanted many, many people to die because of him, not only in his concentration camps but also at the fronts, in the occupied territories, and in Germany itself—tens of thousands every day. Blood, blood must flow—but in his absence. He never visited a bombed German city either, as even his sinister henchman Goebbels at least did. When his train passed through the ruins of a city, the curtains had to be drawn. I think he wanted to be the eye of the hurricane. Around him everything is destroyed, but in the eye the weather is wonderful with blue skies. His villa in the Alps, the Berghof, was the symbol of this. That was where he hatched all those terrors, yet nothing penetrated that idyllic retreat."

"But *why* did he want people to die around him on a massive scale?"

"Perhaps he thought it was a way of warding off his own death. For as long as he could kill, he would stay alive. Perhaps his own death was the only thing he was really afraid of. Perhaps he thought that those huge sacrifices would make him immortal. And in a certain sense, that is what has happened."

"So haven't you already arrived where you want to be? Haven't you grasped everything through your imagination?"

Herter put his pipe in the ashtray and nodded. "There's something in that. Reductio ad absurdum. Right, let me think. So I've already taken a step; the idea is fruitful. But now I want to find something else that is not in conflict with his nature, something that really might have happened but did not happen as far as we know."

"You're sure to find something."

"If anyone can, I can." Herter nodded. He looked at her as a broad smile crossed his face. "Perhaps that's why I'm in the world."

Maria raised her eyebrows. "Are you saying that he has you in his service, too?"

Herter's mood darkened. He crossed his arms and looked at the silent images on the television screen without seeing anything. This was exactly the remark he had not wanted to hear. Sabine, too, had realized that his experiment was a morbid one, but he felt that he already had too strong a hold on the subject to let go. If he were to break all his teeth on it, so be it; he could always get a false set.

A girl in a pristine white Austrian apron appeared with the ice. It rattled as she poured it into the cooler and uncorked the bottle, after which she prepared things for the night in the bedroom. While she was in their suite, they did not talk, as if matters of the greatest secrecy were being discussed that must not be heard even by someone who did not understand their language.

"In fact," said Maria once the brass door handle had risen quietly back into position, "you owe everything you have to your imagination, to something that does not exist in the real world."

"Except for you and Olga, that is. Although . . . maybe even you two. Apart from my children."

"Come on," said Maria, "don't be so timid. Them, too."

"You're right," laughed Herter, turning the bottle around a few times in the cooler. "No beating around the bush. Myself, too."

"And where does it come from? For you it's perfectly normal, but most people haven't an ounce of imagination."

Herter shrugged his shoulders. "Congenital affliction. Like everyone else I am first and foremost a natural phenomenon. It may be connected with the fact that I had no brothers and sisters. I was alone a lot, and my parents were immigrants with few social contacts—none at all with Dutch people. At home everything was different from in Dutch families. In my friends' homes they always said 'Finish your plate,' while my mother had taught me always to leave something—a potato, for example—since otherwise I would give the impression that I had been hungry, and that wasn't chic. I didn't really belong, so I created my own world. Divorced parents—that may be a factor, too. A combination of all that. In any case I never suffered from it. I did not want to belong anywhere. Other people always wanted to belong with *me*—in later life, too."

There was an uncharitable edge to his voice, which did not escape Maria. As she listened, she had been watching the television; now she took the remote off the table and turned on the sound. Rather irritated at her interrupting the conversation like this, Herter watched the nature film, too. Under a lowering African sky, a herd of buffalo was being attacked by jackals; the voice-over said that they had targeted a calf, which they first isolated from its mother. As the calf searched anxiously for its mother and a little later was pounced on and torn apart, Herter said, his face contorted, "Do we have to, Maria?"

Since she did not react immediately, he took the remote from her lap and turned off the television.

She looked at him wide-eyed.

"What did you do that for?"

"I don't want to watch."

"But I do. Don't be so idiotic, it's nature. Give me that thing."

Herter put the remote in his inside pocket.

"I don't need to see it to know that nature is a magnificent failure." He pointed to the gray screen. "That cameraman there should have done only one thing: put his camera on the ground and tried to save the calf. But no—wonderful, wonderful, wonderful, he thought."

"I'm going to bed," said Maria, getting up. "I'm not in the mood for this."

Herter closed his eyes and sighed. Even he did not ultimately understand who he was—but that awareness was not a burden; rather, it gave him a feeling of affirmation. Much to his pleasure, she did not turn on the television in the bedroom; because she had left the door open, he could watch her undress, avoiding looking at him, although she of course knew that he was looking at her. Returning from the bathroom, she slid out of sight under the massive duvet and resumed her reading of a book she had brought from Amsterdam on the problems of gifted children.

Herter put the remote on the table, poured two glasses, and sat close to her on the edge of the bed. As they clinked glasses, they looked at each other in silence for a few seconds, and Herter rested his free hand on Maria's hip.

Maria put her glass on the bedside table, laid her hand on his, and said, "Oh, I forgot to tell you. Yesterday Marnix suddenly asked who Hitler was. He'd picked up something about him. I told him a few things, and then he said, 'Hitler is in hell. But because he likes bad things, it's heaven for him. All Jewish people are in heaven, so that is hell for him. So really he should be in heaven as a punishment.' What do you make of that? Seven years old. You can learn a few things from that."

FOUR

Groaning and complaining that he had become a writer not to produce immortal masterpieces but only so that he could sleep late, Herter got out of bed at eight the following morning. In an hour he would have his first interview. The wine bottle was upside down in the cooler, flanked by another half bottle from the minibar; the festivities had lasted far into the night, the light had not been off for more than five hours. He cursed the pregnant right-hand man, who had made all those appointments, but after a shower and breakfast, which they ate in their room, things improved. When the first journalist knocked, Maria left for the Art History Museum.

The nine-o'clock journalist, the ten-o'clock journalist, and the eleven-o'clock journalist, each accompanied by a photographer, had all seen him on television last night. Their first questions always related to *The Invention of Love*, which they actually turned out to have read, and he did his best to avoid repeating himself. It was unavoidable that he should often say the same things, but it must not happen in the same place and at the same moment; no one read everything, and if there were

25

enough distance in space and time, it could do no harm. Only he himself knew that he had already said this or that spontaneously in Amsterdam, Paris, or London. But all three of them went on to ask about his bright idea of yesterday evening, of placing Hitler in an imaginary situation in order to understand him better. He was not entirely happy about this, as he knew that many of his fellow novelists were thieves and pickpockets, ready to rob him. So, in order to discourage them, he decided to qualify his idea with Maria's argument: that no one could dream up a more extreme situation than the one that Hitler himself had made reality.

At eleven-thirty he concluded the last interview; he had had enough and wanted to go outside. On the front step of the hotel, he breathed in the cold air deeply; it was windy, and he walked down the elegant shopping street to the Stefansdom with his collar turned up and hair waving in the wind. Even now Hitler would not let him alone. Almost a hundred years ago, he had walked here, on his way to the opera to line up for an orchestra ticket for *The Twilight of the Gods*, a down-and-out in threadbare clothes, torn by wild thoughts; perhaps his fanatical eyes had momentarily pierced those of a passing elegant officer of about his own age, the decorated ceremonial saber at his side, monocle in his eye, with Schopenhauer's *Philosophical Aphorisms* in his inside pocket, who was on his way to a romantic assignation at the Sacher. Herter's father perhaps. At the cathedral he turned left and into the Graben. The large space, somewhere between a square and a street, was dominated by the lofty plague column, erected in the seventeenth century to thank God for deliverance from the plague—which had hence been sent by the devil, Herter reflected. He stopped and let his eyes wander over the baroque work of art, which wound its way heavenward like a bronze cypress. The person who had finally put an end to the plague was not God but Alexander Fleming, the discoverer of penicillin; so in fact he deserved a monument as big as St. Peter's in Rome. As he walked on, he thought of Albert Camus's novel *The Plague*, in which the plague stood for the Black Death of National Socialism. The seventeenth-century epidemic cost the lives of thirty thousand Viennese, but two hundred thousand of them died of the six-year Hitler plague and its consequences. Where was the Fleming who could develop an antibiotic against *those* contagious diseases? And where was the grateful monument for the Allied physicians of 1945?

"Germanski niks Kultur," he muttered.

Recognized from the television now and then, he went back to the hotel via a series of narrow streets—the embassy car would be coming in ten minutes to collect them for lunch. As he phoned Maria from the desk to tell her he was waiting downstairs, he saw a famous conductor coming out of the elevator, Constant Ernst, who seldom performed in Holland and whom he knew only by sight. The musician sat down in an armchair, laid a newspaper on his knee, and began rolling a cigarette in the Dutch way without looking at what he was doing. A little later they acknowledged each other with polite nods of the head.

The bewhiskered chauffeur appeared in the lobby at the same time as Maria and looked around inquiringly. When Ernst also gestured and got up, the situation was clear. They approached each other with a smile and shook hands.

"I suppose names are superfluous," said Ernst.

"We are the last two Dutchmen who didn't yet know each other personally."

Ernst had an open smile and two curious eyes behind steel-rimmed glasses. He was ten years younger than Herter, thin, and dressed with superior nonchalance; despite his mustache and the tangled gray hair that hung over his forehead, he made a boyish impression. In the car, next to the driver, he told them that at present he was rehearsing a performance of *Tristan and Isolde* with the Vienna State Opera Orchestra.

"What a perfect coincidence," said Herter, glancing at Maria with a slight shake of the head. "I'm giving a reading tonight." Ernst said nothing about *The Invention of Love*, and it was of course out of the question that either Herter or Maria should ask someone if he had read the book, nor was Maria allowed to do so.

The ambassador's residence was in a grand neighborhood near the Belvedere, bordering the botanical garden. The ambassador and his wife, the Schimmelpennincks, received them standing in the elegantly furnished drawing room, like a living state portrait: the ambassador a thickset gentleman in a dark blue suit with narrow pinstripes, she a simply dressed lady with the kind of smile that generations of mothers and daughters had honed. At their feet lay a shapeless slob of a dog, whose ancestry was an affront to racial purity. When she said that *The Invention of Love* was one of the finest books she had ever read, Herter had the impression that she meant it.

"But we have a terrible confession to make, Mr. Herter," she said, pointing to the dog. "Kees buried your book. Here in the garden." Herter bent down and stroked Kees on the head.

"I saw at once that you're an orthodox Jew," he said.

"What did you say?"

"Religious Jews never throw old books away, nor do they sell them. They bury them. They know how to do things."

Ernst apologized that because of his busy life he had not yet got around to *The Invention of Love*, whereupon Schimmelpenninck helped him out of a tight corner by saying that they already had tickets for his premiere next week. Wagner! Hadn't he, the ambassador asked with an ironic twinkle in the eye, begun his conducting career with the modern Viennese School, with Schoenberg and Webern and Alban Berg? Ernst laughed and said that he still conducted them, but that modernism had precisely begun with Wagner.

"Don't drink too much," whispered Maria as Herter took a glass of white wine from the tray presented to him by an Asian waitress.

"It's the elixir of life."

Schimmelpenninck had seen Herter on television last night and said he was intrigued by his remarks about Hitler.

"What was that, then?" inquired Ernst.

"Mr. Herter is taking on Adolf Hitler," said Schimmelpenninck with a deadpan expression. "The Führer has got it coming to him."

While Schimmelpenninck started explaining the gist, his wife and Maria went off to study the seventeenth-century masters on loan from the Rijksmuseum. Women were no longer interested in Hitler, thought Herter; that used to be different.

When the ambassador had finished, Herter said that Hitler, precisely because of his enigmatic nature, was the dominant twentieth-century figure. Stalin and Mao were also mass murderers, but they were not enigmatic; that was why so much less had been written about them. There had been countless people like them in world history, and there still were and would always be, but there had been only one Hitler. Perhaps he was the most enigmatic human being of all time. That is also why National Socialism had in fact little or nothing to do with the comparatively insignificant fascism of Mussolini or Franco. Wouldn't it be nice if at the conclusion of the twentieth century the last word could be said about him, as a kind of "Final Solution to the Hitler Question"?

"Incidentally," he said, looking at Ernst, "don't take it personally, but a conductor is perhaps the purest example of a dictator."

"Go ahead and say tyrant," said Ernst good-humoredly. "Otherwise it's chaos."

"In fact the word 'conductor' is virtually synonymous with the word 'Führer.' He drills the orchestra, demands total obedience, and his trademark is that he stands with his back to the audience. He is the last to arrive in the auditorium. He receives the applause for a moment, turns his back on the audience, and gives his constant stream of orders. Finally he shows his face again for a moment, basks in the adulation, and is the first to disappear."

"Seems vaguely familiar," said Ernst, and he licked a cigarette paper.

"But Hitler never showed his face. He was a conductor who came onto the platform with his back toward the audience and did not turn around. What I am after now is to hang up something like a fictional mirror, in which we shall be able to see his face after all. I just don't yet know how to approach it."

"Are you never afraid that an idea will come to nothing?" asked Schimmelpenninck cautiously, tugging an earlobe.

"Ideas often come to nothing, but it never worries me. Another idea will come along."

"You have enviable self-confidence."

"If you don't have that, you'll never make it in art."

After that, Ernst told them that that fictional mirror reminded him of what was possibly the oddest experience in his life. About fifteen years ago, he was rehearsing a Mozart symphony in the Felsen Riding School in Salzburg. The musicians were having an off day; he repeatedly had to intervene and make them repeat passages. But suddenly it was as if they were collectively inspired; suddenly they were playing so marvelously that he could not believe his ears. It was as if he were not leading them but they were leading him. When he realized from their eyes that something was going on behind him, he turned around—and what did he see? Herbert von Karajan was standing listening in the doorway of the empty hall.

Herter nodded. "A story like that makes my day."

"And who is standing on *your* threshold, Mr. Herter?" asked Schimmelpenninck with his head cocked to one side.

Herter looked at him in surprise.

"What a good question!" Whom should he name? Goethe? Dostoyevsky? He had the vague feeling that there was a third man, too. "I'm not so sure. If I were a second-rate hack, the answer would be easy."

"I think," said Ernst, "that you are the one standing on the threshold of some other writers."

"In that case I'm saving them a whole lot of work."

They now walked to the dining room. Herter sat on the right of Mrs. Schimmelpenninck, Maria on the ambassador's right. The crockery and the silver cutlery bore the Dutch coat of arms.

"What a coincidence this is," said Mrs. Schimmelpenninck as she was being served. "Mr. Herter writes a novel on the theme of Tristan and Isolde, Mr. Ernst conducts *Tristan and Isolde*, and now they're both sitting down to lunch with us."

"It's not a coincidence at all, dear," said Schimmelpenninck. "On the contrary. Mr. Herter has once again succeeded in shaping reality to his own ends."

"*Je maintiendrai,*" said Herter, pointing to the motto on his plate.

The ambassador raised his glass.

"We'll drink to that."

When Ernst made an appreciative comment on the house, Schimmelpenninck mentioned that Richard Strauss had lived there, and that that was of course no coincidence either. Herter looked around, as if he could still see a ghost somewhere. Here Strauss had sat with Hugo von Hofmannsthal and discussed the latter's libretto for *The Woman Without a Shadow.* Herter himself had also written opera libretti; he knew those kinds of conversations—they were like those of a married couple, with the composer in the role of the wife.

"Strauss is inconceivable without Wagner," Ernst remarked.

Herter fixed him with the look of a detective and asked, "What is the secret of Wagner?"

"His chromaticism," said the conductor without a moment's hesitation. Suddenly he was in his element. "In a certain sense, it points forward to Schoenberg's twelve-tone scale. His endless melodies are never resolved in the tonic as with all previous composers; they constantly brush past it—that is the intoxication of his music, that unfulfilled desire, that delayed gratification."

"So a kind of musical coitus interruptus in fact." Schimmelpenninck nodded.

"Control yourself, Rutger," said his wife.

"I wouldn't dream of it."

"Your husband is quite right, Mrs. Schimmelpenninck. In *Tristan* the eventual harmonic resolution comes only at the end, with the release of death, when there is a black flag waving onstage. There are really only three operas in the world. The first is Monteverdi's *Orfeo*, the second is Mozart's *Don Giovanni*. Wagner was a loathsome individual, an anti-Semite of the first order, but with his *Tristan* he wrote the third."

"Eventual harmonic resolution . . ." repeated Herter slowly, staring at the red meat on his plate. Since cancer had necessitated the removal of his entire stomach, he would be able to eat less than a quarter. He looked up. "You might equally well call it the 'Harmonic Final Solution.' *The Birth of Tragedy from the Spirit of Music*."

FIVE

"That's the title of a book that Nietzsche wrote as a young man in honor of Wagner," he said back in their suite as he took off his jacket. He pulled his tie loose and faltered. "I don't really know what I'm doing. Maybe it's all completely wrong."

"You look rather pale."

"I feel just like the twentieth century. I think I'm going to lie down for a bit. Perhaps that will teach me something."

"Give Marnix a ring first," said Maria as he hung up his jacket. "It's Wednesday, he's home today. He was already asking for you yesterday."

Sitting on the edge of the bed, he dialed the number of Olga, his wife. The moment he heard her voice, he knew she was having a good day: she sounded like a bright spring morning, but it could just as well have been a foggy November afternoon. Her boyfriend, whom she lived with, a cardiologist, had already suggested to him that the University of Amsterdam should set up a chair in Olga Studies. As he took off his shoes, he told Olga how things had gone in Vienna, while she listened patiently, though without great interest. Then his little son came on the line and got straight to the point:

"Daddy, when I die I want to be burned."

"Oh? And why not buried?"

"Then my ashes must be put into that hourglass in your study. That way a person can be of some use forever."

Herter, shocked, was silent.

"Daddy?"

"Yes, I'm still here. So it'll become an ash glass."

"Yes!" laughed Marnix.

"But you're not going to die for a long time yet. You're going to live to be a hundred and ten; you're going to make it into the twenty-second century. By that time the doctors will be able to take care of that."

"They haven't even been born yet!"

"That's right. They'll have to wait for a bit yet."

They talked on for a little, but Herter's mind was distracted. When they had hung up, he told Maria what Marnix had said about his ashes.

"Talk about congenital afflictions . . ." she said, looking at him out of the corner of her eye.

"There is a Chinese saying that goes, 'Great people talk about ideas, medium-level ones about events, and small ones about people.' It's clear which category he belongs in."

"Just as long as it doesn't cause him problems."

Herter looked pensively at the carpet between his feet.

"Literature involves all three, but usually the ideas are missing."

He stretched out on the bed, turned off his hearing aid, and looked at the ceiling. He slowly repeated Marnix's words: "That way a person can be of some use forever. . . ."

"What was that?"

"That was how Marnix put it. Could you write that down? I may be able to use that sentence sometime."

While she did as he had asked, he closed his eyes. Perhaps Marnix would make the twenty-second century, but one day he, too, would be dead, after which the living could measure time forever with his ashes. The ash glass the risen symbol of the mathematically infinite. Eternal, infinite . . . it was all rather long drawn out, but the whole world, the whole spatio-temporal world, was long drawn out. In a hundred years' time the world would be unrecognizable, perhaps even less recognizable than ours would be for people of a hundred years ago. And what will it be like in a thousand years? In ten thousand? A hundred thousand? It was almost inconceivable that that time would come, and yet it would come. Just turn the ash glass again. A million years? Keep counting. Nothing was as patient as numbers. In four or five billion years' time, the sun would swell into a red giant that would swallow up the earth and would then slowly turn to a cinder. Then there would be no more days—but that would be of no importance, because by that time man would have established himself deep in the universe—or at least what had developed from him. Now, approximately halfway through the life of the solar system, you ought to be able to survey in a single moment with the clarity of the present the abysses of the past and future, but how did you reach that moment?

For a second he opened his eyes, as if to make sure that he was still here in Vienna, at the Sacher. In a small armchair by the window, Maria was filing her nails—her image persisted on his retina like a photograph. *Maria, filing her nails; exposure one second.*

He thought of Constant Ernst, who had devoted his life to music. For Herter, too, music had meant more than literature, at least other writers' literature, but that had come to an end when he'd had to sacrifice an essential part of his hearing on the altar of the revolution. In 1967, with scores of other European artists and intellectuals, he had been in Cuba, about which he intended to write a book. For the official commemoration of Fidel's failed attempt at revolution on July 26, 1953, they were flown on the twenty-fifth to Santiago, in the hot province of Oriente on the eastern end of the island. There he started awake at sunrise the following morning to the ear-splitting roar of cannon. For a moment he thought that the American invasion had begun, but it turned out to be salutes, twenty-six of them, fired by an antiaircraft battery stationed right next to the building in which they were accommodated. His ears rang for hours afterward—and three days later, on the night of his fortieth birthday, he suddenly discovered that he had acquired magical powers over nature. If he lay on his right side, he could hear the irrepressible concert of the myriads of crickets in the tropical night, but if he turned over, they were immediately silent. Twenty years later, after his left ear had also been subjected to a trauma, from exploding fireworks, on an icy New Year's Eve, the finer register of his hearing had gone for good. From then on, listening to music gave him as little pleasure as eating.

"That way a person can be of some use forever. . . ." he said softly, without opening his eyes.

He had been in Cuba recovering from "Eichmann syndrome." He had attended the latter's trial in Jerusalem five years before and had written a book about that, too. For weeks, day in and day out, he had listened to the unbearable stories of the Jewish survivors of the extermination camps, while the stage manager of that tragedy seemed to be going slowly mad in his glass cage. His chief, SS artistic director Himmler, had committed suicide, following in the footsteps of the author of that whole chromatic genocide, that inspired maestro in the art of mass murder, whose path Herter had once again crossed— he hoped for the last time. For Herter himself the stupid upshot was that he could no longer fully enjoy not only *Tristan and Isolde* or *Twilight of the Gods* but not even *The Art of Fugue*. Hitler . . . From his cradle to his missing grave, the joy he had spread around him had grown and grown. At his birth only his parents were glad; later he made the whole German people glad, then the Austrian people, too; and when he died, all mankind was glad. . . . He must write this down, or get someone else to. Soon he might forget, but the languid feeling had too strong a hold over him. He started calculating and discovered that by now Hitler had been dead for almost as many years as he had lived. . . . After the disappearance of the Nazi system, Germany and Austria had turned into decently ordered states, while in Russia after the disappearance of the Soviet system, surrealistic anarchism had broken out. Around the corner, in the Balkans, the slaughter had recently returned with a vengeance, albeit in an old-fashioned, preindustrial way, at which Hitler would have shrugged his shoulders; but within a few years that conventional killing spree would have been forgotten.

What was further away: the bloody business in Yugoslavia or the vast exterminations in Auschwitz? Forty-five minutes from Vienna and you were in the Balkans, but the fifty-five years to the Second World War could never be bridged. Yet that war was closer for him, just around the corner in time. . . .

Gradually he was becoming part of the only generation that still had memories of it—insignificant ones compared with the horrors that many others had endured, but nevertheless they were still permeated with the invisible, poisonous gases that, since the National Socialist eruption, had hung in every farthest corner of Europe.

One evening, a little after curfew, he sees himself walking home down a dark street, on tiptoe, close to the houses so as not to be seen; the streetlights have been turned off, and all the windows are blacked out. There is not a sound to be heard. Then, at an intersection in the distance, by the light of the stars, he sees two Home Guards, with helmets and rifles, Dutchmen working for the Germans, walking slowly to and fro and chatting. He dives into a doorway, mouth open and breathing as silently as possible, his heart pounding with fear. . . . That was the war. It was a microscopic facet of what was going on everywhere that evening, in the concentration camps, in the Gestapo cellars, in the bombed cities, at the fronts, at sea—but also petty fear, that the darkness and silence of that moment were *also* a part of that vast stream of exterminating lava pouring forth from the Hitler crater and flooding Europe, and it could not be explained to those born later. . . . That creature had failed at everything, first as an artist in Vienna and then as a politician in Berlin; he wanted to eradicate Bolshevism, but he lured it into the heart of Germany; he wanted to exterminate the Jews, but he initiated the state of Israel. He had succeeded in dragging 55 million people to their deaths with him—and perhaps that was precisely his intention. If he had had a way of blowing up the world, he would have used it. Death was the dominant theme in his essence. How could Herter investigate to see if there were some last grain of love of life in that mortal? Something to do with his favorite dog perhaps? Or Eva Braun, whom he married at the last moment? Why? How could Herter set up a laboratory experiment to put Hitler under high pressure, so that he was forced to show his full face straight on? . . . A mirror, he had said to Ernst. A mirror machine . . . His breathing slows. He is sitting at the edge of a large pond with Olga; she is showing him photos, but she is dazzled by the bright sunlight on the water. . . . Suddenly he is violently abducted by a man and a boy. . . . When he sees the room in which they imprison him, he cries, "Yes, this is where I want to live." . . . That embarrasses them, but they cannot go back, so that they have become *his* prisoners. . . .

·SIX

"Have you done some preparation for this?" asked Maria in the elevator.

"Of course. You saw me sleeping, didn't you?"

"Have you got your book with you?"

"They're bound to have it there."

At six in the café of the Sacher, he had a preliminary discussion with the president of the organizing Austrian literary society, Mrs. Klinger, and with a critic, a very earnest young man, who introduced himself as "Marte." He had closely cropped hair, a silver ring in his left earlobe, and over his shoulder he carried a kind of game bag full of papers. When Herter also saw a copy of *The Invention of Love* in German, he asked if he might use it later. There was not much to discuss; things would proceed as they always did: after the introduction he would say a few things about his novel, read for about three-quarters of an hour, after which the audience under the chairmanship of Marte could ask questions. Herter asked him if he would repeat each question briefly, as he was a little "gun deaf," as it was called in military circles. Would Herter rather stand or sit? He preferred to sit. What would he like to drink? Water please, still. There would also be a book stand—was he prepared to sign? Of course he was prepared to sign. Writing was his greatest pleasure in life, he said. Following the lecture there would be a buffet reception.

After half an hour, a boyish-looking man in his forties appeared, who with his red hair and pale skin resembled an Irishman but introduced himself in melting Viennese as the manager of the Sacher. It was an honor for him to shake the hand of Herr Doktor Herter, and he asked if he might be so bold as to drive them to the National Library; it was ten minutes' walk away, on the Josefplatz, but the weather was bad, and he himself wanted to attend the reading.

Outside the door stood the hotel's Rolls-Royce, the same brown color as the famous cake. Because he did not feel like talking, Herter sat next to the chauffeur. Apart from a group of inveterate Herter haters in his own country, everyone was behaving more and more nicely to him as he got older, but, aware that no one really knew who he was, he preferred to be at home in his study, alone, without appointments, without telephone, the day extending before him virgin and untouched. Even when he had had to go to school every morning, he experienced it as something that kept him from his real activities, but the teachers concluded from his poor marks that he was lazy and stupid and would come to no good. Fortunately they had been able to see, a number of years later, that he was the reverse of lazy, and moreover, see which of them was really stupid: he or they. No one had ever heard another word about all those bright pupils that they had held up to him with a shake of their heads as examples.

The National Library was part of the Hofburg, the great imperial complex of palaces and government buildings, from where for centuries a world empire had been ruled, before it had turned into the hydrocephalic head of a dwarf. At the entrance to the library, under the umbrella that the driver held above his head, Herter was welcomed by the director, Herr Doktor Lichtwitz, who led him up marble staircases to the colossal baroque reception room, the most august location in Austria. Schimmelpenninck was there again, and in some strange way the pinstripes on his dark blue suit had disappeared. Under the exuberantly painted dome sat several hundred people; but because extra chairs were constantly being brought in through a side entrance, they waited until everyone had found a seat.

As he entered, there was applause, and, as always, he found it difficult to look at the hundreds of faces turned in his direction, precisely because he could not register a single individual face. He knew that all of those here had devoted a few hours of their lives to his books. It embarrassed him—and perhaps, he reflected as he allowed himself to be led to his reserved chair in the middle of the front row, it was what distinguished him from Hitler, who was precisely in his element when confronted with such an anonymous mass: the element of his own individuality, which was the only one that counted in confrontation with all those hundreds, thousands, millions, that he was prepared to hound to their deaths. Herter realized he was at work again, but not on what he had been invited here for. What he would have most liked to do was to leave the auditorium and make notes in the hotel.

After an introduction by Schimmelpenninck, who praised

him as Holland's cultural ambassador, Lichtwitz compared him to Hugo de Groot—or "Grotius," as he called him. Herter looked up in surprise. He had already been compared to Homer, Dante, Milton, and Goethe, but Hugo de Groot was new. In order to put it in perspective, he made a brief, aristocratic military salute, with his hand slightly bent, like his father in photographs from the First World War. He knew that that gesture was risky, that it robbed the audience of some of the reverence they needed—but besides that, he knew he was lost if he ever started seeing himself in all earnestness as a second Homer, Dante, Milton, Goethe, or Hugo de Groot. There was only one person with whom he must continue to identify with, if he wanted to survive, and that was the boy behind the frost flowers that he had once been. Hitler on the other hand, the absolutist, modeled himself on Alexander the Great, Julius Caesar, Charlemagne, Frederick the Great, and Napoleon, while his youth might just as well never have existed.

Mrs. Klinger also was proud of their guest. She listed a number of his awards and prizes, mentioned the honorary citizenship of his hometown, his membership here in Austria in the Academia Scientiarum et Artium Europaea, and told them that he had been published in thirty countries, including China. After briefly discussing a few of his best-known books, she reminded the audience of his Viennese family origins.

"The great Dutch author Rudolf Herter belongs to us, too, in a small way," she concluded. "The floor is yours."

She could not have made it more difficult for him. As he got up, he wobbled slightly, which he deftly disguised, but of course everyone had seen it anyway, if only from Maria's outstretched hand. The critic passed him his novel, after which he sat down at a table between the columns and the life-size marble statues and took in the scene opposite him for a few seconds. In the horizontal plane, the many hundreds of faces; behind, twenty yards high, interrupted by a gallery, the thousands of precious volumes from the Habsburg library. There had been many high points in his life, but he experienced this as one of the most spectacular: if only his father could see him now.

When he began to speak, his tiredness and distractedness vanished instantly. He told the audience something of the long gestation of *The Invention of Love* and the role of the Tristan legend in it, which he had interwoven with certain personal experiences. Exactly which experiences must of course remain a secret, since if he were to revisit them, he would have written for nothing. For him there were still those two worlds, each as real as the other: the world of his individual experiences and the world of mythical stories; they must create something like a chemical reaction with each other and form a new compound—only then was the kind of book that he wanted to write produced. He regarded his study as the no-man's-land between those two worlds. When he saw that some of the audience were taking notes, he was about to say that they should not do so, because if they were to forget what he said, it couldn't have been any good; but that might create the impression that he wanted a cheap laugh at the expense of those good souls. He got his laugh a little later anyway, when he opened *The Invention of Love* and said he was going to read a chapter but that he hadn't written a word of it himself, as it was a translation.

The novel had been out of his system for a few years, like an illness that had been overcome; since then he had published other titles, but still he stumbled every few minutes over a

47

word or expression that did not exactly render what the Dutch said. His memory of the events in his life was poor rather than good, and he was repeatedly forced to ask Maria or Olga what something had been like—but if he saw a passage quoted from something he had written fifty years ago and there was a period somewhere instead of a semicolon, he saw it immediately. No way would he have put a period there! Or the absence of an exclamation mark. When he checked, it turned out that he was never wrong. If all his books were to vanish from the face of the earth as a result of a dreadful natural phenomenon, he would be able to reconstruct them all word for word, from A to Z, in a short space of time. Given unlimited time, anyone could of course write them, and all other books, too, even the unwritten ones.

In order to keep visual contact with the audience, he looked up briefly from his text now and then. He had to force himself, and each time it gave him a little jolt as he realized he was the focus of all those eyes and rapt faces. They were hanging on his every word, they were all absorbed in the scene he was reading—and each of them mastered an art that he himself could not master: that of listening. Even at school, long ago, in the war, the words of the teachers did not get through to him, since he was totally absorbed by looking at them, at their body language, the skin of their hands, how they wore their hair, the way they had knotted their tie, and at anything else that was happening in the classroom: the behavior of the other pupils, the fly on the top window, the waving of the leaves on the trees, the clouds scudding past. . . . "Pay attention, Rudi!"—yet he was paying not too little but too much attention. The result was that he had to study everything again at home that his classmates already knew after the lesson. That was no problem in itself—dyslexia was the last thing he suffered from. The problem was just that at home he preferred to read books that really interested him. This in turn led to weeks of playing hooky, and finally he was kicked out of the school, which was absolutely fine by him, because he was just wasting his time. "Aural dyslexia" was what he tended to call his defect. That syndrome, identical with his talent, of course, also underlay his lifelong inability to follow a lecture, a play, or even a simple thriller on television. As the patrol car roared down the hilly streets of San Francisco with its siren wailing, his attention was focused not on the exciting story, which he never understood, but on a woman who just happened to be strolling down the sidewalk blissfully unaware of what was to come. Who was she? Where was she going? Was she still alive? The only situation in which he was capable of listening was when someone addressed him personally.

After the applause Marte sat down beside him and asked, to get things started, why he had put the dream in the passage he had read aloud in the present tense, when, apart from that, the novel was written in the past tense. That was of course a good question, and the young man with the ring in his ear rose in his estimation. Herter replied that he had always done that with dreams, for as long as he could remember, since dreams, just like myths, were ahistorical in nature. You did not say "Tristan loved Isolde" but "Tristan loves Isolde."

"Apart from that," he said, running both hands through his hair, "I cannot say for sure, and there are others who know better than I do, but it is possible that I have never written a novel without a dream in it. A novel or a story is nothing but a consciously constructed dream. A novel without a dream runs counter not only to human beings, who both wake and sleep, but also to the nature of the novel."

Virtually without exception the questions from the audience, which Marte repeated each time, were ones he had answered before, in countless cities in Europe and America. On the few occasions when he could not think of a good reply, he answered a question that had not been put, which invariably proved satisfactory.

"Thomas Mann," he said when a distinguished gentleman stood up and asked him whom he regarded as his literary father.

"And your literary grandparents?"

"Goethe and Dostoyevsky," he said immediately, thinking about his four literary great-grandparents, who of course might come next.

"And your literary son?"

He burst out laughing. "You've got me there. I don't know."

The director seized the moment of mirth to thank him, after which he walked with Maria to the trestle table with his translated books on it.

"Did it go okay?" he inquired.

"Has it ever gone badly?"

"There's no need for you to stay here," he said, sitting down and unscrewing the top of his fountain pen. "Why don't you go and keep Mrs. Schimmelpenninck company?" There was already a line, and he saw the curiosity with which people looked at Maria, too, especially women: Why her? What kind of woman was she? Wasn't she thirty years younger? In what ways did she know him? What was he like in bed?

Now he finally had the chance to look directly at everyone,

although there were some who avoided his eyes. With each new look he had forgotten the last, but he knew that they would remember his. Almost everyone who handed him a book had opened it at the flyleaf, where the person's own name belonged; he turned another page and signed it on the actual title page. If someone asked him to write a name in it, of the person for whom the book was intended, he did so—but there were some people who placed a piece of paper in front of him with something like "For Ilse, with love always." Then he sometimes had difficulty in explaining that he was sure he would love Ilse if he knew her, but that, sadly, was not the case. Occasionally that cost him an angry look. And then there were always those who set a briefcase on the table and took out ten books: would he please sign them, with a dedication, date, and place? In those instances he would point to the long line of people waiting and say that he could not do that to the others. After half an hour came the inevitable moment when his hand had forgotten how to write his name and could produce only a trembling caricature of it, like an incompetent forger.

Nevertheless, after Maria had placed a second glass of white wine next to him, the end was in sight. But when he had screwed the top back on his fountain pen and was about to stand up, two little old people approached, husband and wife, whom he had seen standing there before. Obviously they had waited until they were the last. The man made a humble bow and asked in laborious Dutch, with a heavy German accent, "Mr. Herter, could we speak to you briefly for a moment?"

SEVEN

"Of course," said Herter, also in Dutch. He had just about had enough, but he did not want to disappoint them. "And feel free to speak German," he added in German.

"Thank you, Mr. Herter."

They looked around rather helplessly.

"Please have a seat."

Herter shot a glance at the bookseller, who was already packing up but immediately took the hint. The couple must have been nearer ninety than eighty and looked impoverished but well groomed. Everything the old gentleman was wearing was beige—his shirt, his tie, his suit—combined with light gray shoes. Someone had obviously persuaded him that this look made a brighter impression at his age. His collar, which was too wide for him, indicated that he had shrunk a couple of sizes. He was bald and at the same time not bald; his white hair lay across his pale scalp, which had pink patches here and there, like a transparent haze. She was as fat as he was thin: it was as if she had absorbed him almost completely. Her face, framed by small gray curls, was broad and slightly Slavic and further accented by gold-colored spectacles with outsize lenses; her cheeks still had a flush, which looked natural.

When they had sat down, they introduced themselves as Ullrich and Julia Falk. Her hand was hot, his as cool and dry as paper.

"This is a very difficult moment for us, Mr. Herter," said Mr. Falk. "We discussed for a long time whether we should do this. We've never even attended a reading like this before. . . ."

He did not know how to handle this, and, to put them at their ease, Herter said, "I'm happy you came at any rate."

Falk glanced at his wife, who nodded at him.

"We saw you on television last night, Mr. Herter. Quite by accident, because we never watch that kind of program. They're not meant for people like us. But then you suddenly said something about Hitler. It was over very quickly, and we're not sure if we understood you correctly."

"I'm sure you did."

"You said that Hitler is becoming more and more incomprehensible. And then you said something about the imagination. That you want to catch him with the imagination."

Julia nodded. "In a net."

"That was exactly what I said."

Falk glanced at Herter. A sharp expression had appeared in his blue eyes. "Perhaps we can help you."

Flabbergasted, Herter returned his look. He did not really know what to say. "With imagination?"

"No, you don't need any help with that. With something real. To show you what he was like."

Suddenly relations were reversed. Suddenly he was no longer sitting there as the great writer in a magnificent hall, opposite a simple, hesitant couple, but had himself become the uncertain one.

"Mr. Falk, you're making me very curious." He looked around. In the empty auditorium, men were clearing away the chairs, at the stall the remaining books were already in cardboard boxes, and a little farther away, Maria, Lichtwitz, and the Schimmelpennincks were waiting for him. "I'm a guest here, and I have obligations now. Can't we meet somewhere tomorrow?"

"Where are you staying?" asked Falk hesitantly. "Of course we could come to your hotel tomorrow."

"Out of the question. You've already taken enough trouble. I'll come to you."

Falk looked doubtfully at his wife; when she nodded and at the same time shrugged her shoulders briefly, he agreed. They lived in an old-people's home, Eben Haëzer. Herter noted the address and the number of their flat, got up, and shook hands. He would come for coffee at ten-thirty tomorrow.

"What did that old couple want?" asked Maria, when he joined the others.

"They know something," said Herter after he had told her. "They know something that no one knows."

The cocktail reception was held in a side room. There were thirty or forty guests from the Viennese literary world, who did not give the impression of having missed him. He would have preferred to drink a glass of wine and eat something in a corner, but there was no way of escaping being introduced to all these writers, poets, critics, publishers, and editors. Actually he did not want to meet anyone else; he felt that he knew enough people by now. Apart from that, he had instantly forgotten their names and functions when they were introduced, since he was too preoccupied with looking at people and sounding them out. It was not unknown for him to introduce himself three or four times to the same person, from which the person concluded that he really was going senile—but it was worse than that: ultimately he was not interested in who was who or what. Both in *The Invention of Love* and in other novels, he had evoked figures that had moved many readers, yet for himself other people—apart from the twenty or thirty people closest to him—counted only to the extent that he could fit them into his imaginative world. But perhaps that rather inhuman, almost autistic quality was precisely the precondition for creating those characters. Perhaps the foundation of all art was a certain relentlessness, which was better hidden from good-natured art lovers.

"You're not really with it," said Maria when he was finally left in peace.

"That's right. I want to get out of here."

"Yes, and you can't. This has been organized for you, by all kinds of nice people. You'll have to sacrifice yourself for a little longer."

He nodded. "It's just as well I have an obedient nature and am self-effacing."

A small, plump woman made a beeline for him and clasped his hands with both of hers, beginning to shake them effusively, gazing at him with shining eyes.

"Mr. Herter, thank you, thank you for your wonderful book. *The Invention of Love* is the finest novel I have ever read. I put off reading the final pages for days because I did not want it to end—as far as I'm concerned, it could have been a thousand pages longer. I immediately started reading it again. That's why I was so glad that you remarked in your introduction that you need the end before the beginning." She did not wait for an answer; she turned on her heel blushing, and it was as if she were taking flight.

"The terrible things I do to people," said Herter.

Half an hour later, the manager of the Sacher appeared: he was ready to drive them back to the hotel at any moment. For Herter this was the signal that he could leave with decorum; he refused the offer with thanks, preferring to walk and get a breath of fresh air.

"Are you sure? A storm has been forecast."

"I'm sure."

Saying his good-byes took almost another half an hour. Lichtwitz accompanied them to the exit and impressed on Herter that he must be sure to let him know when he was next in Vienna.

In the square they were caught unawares by a vortex of strange gusting winds, which seemed to come from all directions. The sky was as dark as the back of a mirror, and now and then Herter felt a stray raindrop in his face. As he apologized to Maria for having to leave her alone tomorrow, through Hitler's fault, the wind gradually grew stronger—and suddenly a blast of such force that they could scarcely keep upright came straight down the Augustinerstrasse toward them. There was a roaring and clattering everywhere. Shutters swung open and banged against the walls, windows shattered, and planters and cycles toppled, followed a few seconds later by a blinding, mountainous cloud of dust and grit. Rubbing their eyes, with their backs to the storm, they stopped. There were flashes of lightning, ear-shattering thunderclaps reverberated through the city, and a moment later a cloudburst of such ferocity exploded that it was as if they were standing under the shower fully dressed.

"Pay no attention!" shouted Herter, leaning at an angle into the wind and continuing. "Pretend you don't notice it! Show it who's boss!"

EIGHT

The next morning at breakfast, their eyes were still irritated by the dust. Maria was going to view the Dürer in the Albertina, and they would see each other for lunch.

"If it gets any later, make your own arrangements," said Herter. "The plane doesn't leave till eight-thirty tonight."

It was calm autumn weather. On the way to the taxi stand, with a copy of *The Invention of Love* under his arm, he bought a bunch of flowers for Mrs. Falk. He thought back to his reading of the previous evening. It was so definitively over that it was as if it had never taken place. He had given hundreds of such readings in his life, at first for the top classes of secondary schools, to which he had to go by train and bus, later for cultural societies and universities, to which he drove in his own car, and finally only for prestigious gatherings at home and abroad, which laid on airplanes, limousines, and five-star hotels. The following day it was always over so finally that it might never have happened. Time was a maw without a body—a maw that devoured everything, grinding it all up without a trace.

As he opened the door of the taxi, he was met by piano music.

"Satie," he said as they drove off, *"Gymnopédie."* The pianist's touch was crude, and the tempo was too fast. "Is it the radio or a tape?" he asked.

"A tape."

"Who's playing?"

The driver, a fat chap in his twenties, glanced at him in the mirror. "My father."

"Really? Not bad."

"He died three months ago," said the driver, this time without looking at him.

Herter sighed. How could one not love mankind? Here an anonymous Viennese taxi driver was listening to the piano playing of his dead father, which he had doubtless taped himself.

"Now I take over," said the driver. There was a moment's silence, after which it continued in virtually the same way.

Not only was there not a leaf left on the trees, but all over the city, trees that had blown down were being transformed by whining circular saws into stacks of dead wood. What on earth was one to make of it? Herter wondered. On the one hand you had this heartrending driver, on the other the most blood-thirsty rabble—how in heaven's name could one reconcile the two? All cows were like all other cows, all tigers like all other tigers—what on earth has happened to human beings? Listening to the music, which overused the pedal, he was driven through shabby neighborhoods where he had never been before. The Eben Haëzer old-people's home, a large, blackened six-story building from the beginning of the twentieth century, was in a bleak street on the edge of town, behind a station.

Here and there in the tiled hall, old people in dressing gowns were sitting on wooden benches, their sticks beside them, feet in slippers. Herter reported to the desk, where he was told that, because of rebuilding work, he must first take the elevator to the fourth floor, turn left, and at the end of the corridor take the elevator back to the third floor, then turn right down the corridor. As he walked along the worn carpet of the endless corridor on the fourth floor, down which an ancient woman was shuffling, holding the railing that had been fitted along its whole length, Herter was astonished that his life had brought him back here of all places, under one roof with a centenarian in a Vienna suburb.

Falk

Ullrich Falk, small, in a baggy cardigan, again beige, opened the door.

"Welcome, Mr. Herter. What an honor."

The whole apartment was less than half the size of Herter's study in Amsterdam. It smelled stuffy and musty; the windows had not been opened for months or years. Only the smell of fresh coffee made some amends. In the tiny kitchen, where they obviously also ate, Julia poured a stream of hot water from a whistling kettle into a brown coffeepot with a filter—a model that he had not seen since his youth. Blushing, she received the flowers; it was clear that such a thing had not happened to her for a very long time. He glanced sideways into their bedroom, the door of which was half open: the space was scarcely larger than the bed. In the living room, there was just room for a sofa, a small armchair, and a couple of cabinets full of knickknacks. In the corner was an ancient television set; on top of it was a framed photograph of a blond boy, four or five years old, with a smiling young woman next to him, obviously his mother. Perhaps it was their grandson, or great-grandson. Herter sat down on the dull green sofa, the worn arms of which were covered with pieces of material that themselves belonged in the trash can. Above it hung a framed reproduction of Brueghel's *Peasant Wedding*.

"To tell you the truth, Mr. Herter," said Falk, with *The Invention of Love* on his lap, "we didn't think you would come. You, such a famous writer—"

"Nonsense," Herter interrupted him. "That famous writer is nothing to do with me."

Apologizing for the fact that they had no vase, Julia put the flowers in a red plastic bucket on the low table. After she had poured the weak coffee and presented crumbly sponge cake, she sat down next to him on the sofa and lit up a cigarette; blowing out the match, she put it back in the box. Herter could see that they were not at ease; he decided to control his impatience and asked if they had always lived in Vienna. They looked at each other for a moment.

"Almost always," said Falk.

Herter felt that he must not probe any further. "How old are you, if I may ask?"

"I was born in 1910, my wife in 1914."

"So you have lived through almost the whole century."

"It wasn't a very wonderful century."

"But it was an interesting one. At least for those who have lived to tell the tale. Let's say that it was an unforgettable century."

In reply to Herter's question about his background, Falk told him that his father had been a baker's assistant at Dehmel on the Kohlmarkt. He had scarcely known him: he had been killed in the First World War on the Somme, after which Falk's mother earned her living as a cleaner for rich families on the Ringstrasse. He had gotten no further than primary school. He found a job as a postman, and, while working for the post office, he followed a course at the secondary hotel school, as he wanted to do better in life than his father. By the time he gained his diploma at the age of twenty, his mother had already died.

"And so you became a headwaiter."

"Among other things."

"What else, then?"

Falk looked at him out of the corner of his eye. "A Nazi."

Herter burst out laughing, so that some crumbs of sponge cake flew out of his mouth. "That must have been a strange school."

But it was not through the school. He changed jobs a few times, and in 1933—the year when Hitler came to power in Germany—he found work in a café frequented by right-wing radicals of the recently banned Nazi Party, as happened in countless places in Austria under the direction of NSDAP headquarters in Munich. Using a card club as cover, they made their revolutionary plans in a back room full of cigar smoke, with their cards on the table in front of them. Even Dr. Arthur Seyss-Inquart was present on one occasion, a lawyer who was to become Austrian chancellor and was to ask Hitler formally to annex Austria.

"And who two years later was rewarded by being appointed commissioner of the occupied Netherlands," added Herter, "but by then I expect he had disappeared from your horizon. For what he got up to with us, especially with the Jews, he was hanged at Nuremberg."

"I know," said Falk. "For the last six months of the war, we worked in his household, in The Hague."

Herter looked at him in astonishment but suppressed his inclination to ask him more questions. "Well, then you know all the gentlemen. Like Rauter, the supreme commander of the SS and the police in the Netherlands, also a compatriot of yours. Looked at closely, we were actually occupied by Austria. All Vienna's finest, if I can put it like that. Sometimes I think that the annexation of Austria by Germany was in fact an annexation of Germany by Austria. And in the same year of 1892, all those Austrians were lying as delightful babies at their mothers' breasts—Seyss, Rauter, down to my own father, who didn't behave too well in the war either. I simply mention this for the record." He was about to add ". . . so that you don't feel guilty," but he swallowed the remark; it remained to be seen how guilty Falk should feel.

Falk was silent for a moment and exchanged a glance with Julia, who stubbed out her cigarette in the ashtray. Politics did not interest him, he continued; to begin with, it meant nothing to him—his job was to put beer and wine and sausage on the table. But that changed when he met Julia.

"Yes, blame it on me," said Julia. It was the first time that she had joined in the conversation. In a stagy way, she tried to create the impression that she was indignant, but the look in her eyes said something different. With a motion of the head, she pointed to her Ullrich. "Look at him sitting there. You won't believe it, but in those days he was a golden blond Germanic god, four inches taller than he is now, straight as a die, and with big blue eyes. I fell for him right away."

She was the daughter of one of the fascist leaders, a bookkeeper in the municipal transport company; one evening she met him after work—and what do you know, they'd been together for sixty-six years. Ullrich came regularly to her house, where her father gave him *Mein Kampf* to read and in no time won him over to National Socialist thinking.

"These days it is all seen from the perspective of Auschwitz," said Falk apologetically, "but that didn't exist at that time. I looked at it from the perspective of that miserable Austria of Dollfuss, in which my mother had to work herself to death."

Herter nodded in silence. Falk knew how to build up his story, beginning with the background to what really concerned him. He had obviously prepared.

He married Julia and no longer participated only as a waiter in the illegal meetings, designed to put an end to Austria. A year later, in July 1934, he took part in a risky armed-coup attempt in the Chancellery, in which Dollfuss was murdered—a day of blunders and misunderstandings on both sides. In the complete confusion he was able to escape and avoid his punishment.

Two years later, in 1936, his career unexpectedly took off. One spring day, wearing a crumpled suit, one of Hitler's adjutants appeared at a subversive evening of cards in the café. He explained that there was a vacancy at Hitler's country home, the Berghof, for an experienced waiter-cum-butler, whose wife could work in the household. Everyone immediately looked his way. That summer, after the Gestapo in Munich had checked their backgrounds—in collaboration with the Austrian police, of course—and after the Registry Office had confirmed that they were of pure Aryan blood, Ullrich and Julia boarded the train and traveled to Berchtesgaden.

"No small matter," said Herter. "Weren't you trembling with fear?"

"Fear . . . fear . . ." repeated Falk. "There wasn't so much cause for that at the time. The real nightmare was still to come. For us, too. At that moment I was mainly relieved to be able to get out of Austria, as it was still possible they might discover that I had taken part in the coup. There was a minimum sentence of fifteen years for that. Dollfuss had been canonized. I might even be strung up."

"It was as if we had stumbled into a dream," said Julia. "I don't know if you've ever been there, but . . . Today everyone vacations abroad at least two or three times a year, but we had never been out of Vienna, and suddenly we were standing there in that fairy-tale alpine landscape. In fine weather you could see Salzburg in the distance."

"Hitler liked that bit of Germany because it's actually Austria," said Falk. "Even at the beginning of the 1920s, he went there regularly to relax and think. If you look on the map, you can see that it sticks into Austria like . . . like . . ."

Like a penis, Herter was going to add, but he said, "It was obviously something like his ideal place. He recognized himself in that romantic wilderness more than in the modern traffic jams of Munich or Berlin. Perhaps everyone has such an absolute spot. What would yours be, Mrs. Falk?"

When she did not immediately understand what he meant, Falk said, "We haven't seen that much of the world, Mr. Herter. We're just ordinary people. What about you?"

Herter looked at the ceiling, at a brown damp patch in the shape of a hedgehog. "Perhaps in Egypt, in that special piece of desert where the pyramids and the Sphinx are."

The adjutant, Krause, now in a tight-fitting black SS uniform, picked them up from the station in a car and took them past a series of barriers and sentry posts to the Obersalzberg.

They were not yet shown the actual villa, designed by Hitler himself. Behind it, not visible from the road, was a huge complex of barracks, bunkers, firing ranges, garages, a hotel for high-ranking guests, barracks for workers, staff housing, even a nursery school; everywhere, day and night, building continued, and roads were being constructed. In a block of flats, where the other domestic staff also lived, they were assigned a small apartment. In the office of the majordomo, SS Lieutenant General Brückner, a huge old warhorse who had taken part in Hitler's failed coup in Munich in 1923, they had to swear an oath of secrecy to the Führer regarding everything they heard or saw at the Berghof; nor were they allowed to keep a diary. If they were to break that oath, at the very least they would face a concentration camp.

So he is going to break that oath after more than sixty years, thought Herter. He said nothing, but Falk had read his thoughts.

"I don't know whether an oath applies beyond the grave. Now that all those people are dead, a lot has come to light. But not everything." Falk looked for words. "I don't know if such a thing is possible, but we'd like you to take over the oath from us. At least for the little time we have left; afterward you can do what you like with it. It's something we don't want to take with us to our graves."

"I accept," swore Herter with his fingers raised—realizing that he had now entered a satanic domain: the oath linked him to Falk, just as it had linked Falk to Hitler himself.

NINE

"When was the first time you saw him?" he asked Falk, giving Julia another light.

"Not until a week later. He was in Berlin at the Chancellery. We were introduced to Miss Braun the next day, though."

"The lady of the house."

"We didn't know that at the time," said Julia. "Almost no one knew, only a very small circle. She was supposedly one of his secretaries, but everyone referred to her as the 'Lady Chief.' After a few days, when I had to take up her breakfast and the morning newspaper, I saw what things were really like. The secretaries all lived elsewhere on the site—"

"Much to the pleasure of the SS officers," interjected Falk.

"And not forgetting Bormann." Julia's face still expressed contempt. "But her bedroom was in the Berghof itself, on the first floor, and separated from Hitler's only by a shared bathroom."

Miss Braun was a lonely, unhappy creature, who must be kept hidden for political reasons, since the Chief wanted to belong to all German women. A peroxided, pretty, sporty woman of twenty-four, always good humored in company, she was two years older than Julia, with whom she was immediately on excellent terms. She was alone a lot; sometimes she did nothing for weeks on end except read novels, play records, and keep her diary up to date. As there was no one else she could talk to, she soon took Julia into her confidence. When the Chief was not there, they would secretly smoke cigarettes, flat Egyptian ones, Stambul brand; if Hitler had known that Miss Eva smoked, he would have put an immediate end to their relationship. Even in winter they opened the window wide, since one of the SS bodyguards might smell it and report it to Brückner, who might mention it to Bormann, who would definitely see to it that the Chief got to hear. Head of Chancellery Bormann was his powerful, half-anonymous secretary, who controlled his diary and his finances. Miss Braun hated him. In her opinion that big-boned fellow on whose arm she always had to go from the great hall to the dining room in company, had far too much influence on her Adi—while he in turn disliked her because she escaped his control. But he knew how to make himself indispensable. Once the Chief had complained that during the periodical parades of admirers—many of them women—he often found the sun a problem, the following day a tree with thick foliage was standing there. On another occasion he had remarked that a farmhouse in the distance actually spoiled the pristine quality of the view—the following day the farmhouse was gone.

Yes, thought Herter, that is absolute power. He did not need to give Bormann any orders to have it done; he had the kind of power over people that others have only over their own bodies. If someone wants to take a glass off the table, he does not have to order his hand to do so first: he simply does it. Compared with Hitler, everyone was paralyzed.

Miss Braun had known Hitler since she was seventeen, even before he assumed power, when she worked in the shop of Hitler's personal photographer, Heinrich Hoffmann; she had once told Julia that she liked working in the darkroom best. Her work in the photographic archive had obviously led to the strange habit of keeping a meticulous record of her extensive wardrobe, with detailed descriptions, drawings, and attached samples of material. Anyway, she changed outfits four or five times a day, even when there was no reason at all. She liked sunbathing, but the Chief had banned that, too, since he disliked tanned skin. Hitler, interrupted Falk, hated the sun. Even in summer he always wore his uniform cap or a hat. The Berghof lay on the north slope of a huge alp, so that in the winter it was already bitterly cold by afternoon, and that was of course intentional. In the new Chancellery in Berlin, his rooms also faced north. He could not stand bright electric light either. There was never more than a single table lamp. He did not wish to be photographed with a flash.

The Enemy of Light, thought Herter—might that be a suitable title for his story? Or why not go the whole hog: *The Prince of Darkness*? No, that was too much of a good thing.

In those Munich days, Miss Braun confided to Julia, Hitler had an affair with his niece, who committed suicide when he had a short flirtation with Eva. Four out of five other girl-friends of his had made suicide attempts, but only this one had succeeded. Hitler had wanted to do away with himself, too, at the time, Falk had once heard from the mouth of Rudolf Hess, at the time his deputy, who had to wrench the pistol from his hand. Around the Berghof it was whispered that his niece was pregnant at the time; whatever the truth of this, he had become a vegetarian from then on. So that, thought Herter, was the reaction of a necrophiliac. Every day Julia had to place fresh flowers by the niece's portrait in the great reception room. During that period, when because of his hectic schedule he neglected her for months, Miss Braun had also clumsily shot a bullet into her neck, which bound him to her forever. For that matter, a year before she herself arrived at the Berghof, Miss Braun had made a second suicide attempt in Munich for the same reason, after which he had her move in with him on the Obersalzberg.

"So he was capable of love," Herter said, nodding, "but at the same time, even in his private life he exuded death."

"I don't know if it was love," said Falk with a deadpan expression.

"Wasn't there a grain of goodness in him somewhere?"

"No."

"He loved his dog."

"At the end he tried out the poison on it, before giving it to Miss Braun."

"But Miss Braun was capable of love," said Julia. "If he was not at the Berghof and she had to eat alone, she always wanted me to put his photo by her plate."

Herter remained looking at her in silence for a moment, while he saw the scene before him: that lonely woman at the table with the portrait of her lover, through whose agency hundreds were already dying, a bit later thousands, and finally millions.

"But she ate very little and irregularly," said Falk. "In fact, after meals she always took a purgative. She was terrified of becoming fat."

"So that means she suffered from anorexia; but maybe the symptoms were not familiar at the time. And Hitler himself? What was your first impression of the Führer?"

Falk paid no attention to the ironic note with which he spoke the word "Führer." His eyes wandered to the window, which looked out over a neglected courtyard. There was something there that only he could see. The rather sleepy passing of the days, in which he had been shown the ropes at the Berghof, had given way to a nervous, agitated atmosphere. In the afternoon a column of open Mercedeses appeared in the drive and stopped in front of the formal steps. It was as if, said Falk—and he knew that it could not be explained—everything had suddenly gone icy cold and frozen. Through a kitchen window he saw Hitler getting out and looking around for a moment at the overwhelming alpine panorama, while he pulled his belt down a little with a slight tug. The peak of his uniform cap was larger than those of the others and was also farther over his eyes. There he stood, the Führer, exactly where he stood and nowhere else. He was smaller than Falk had imagined. His body language, at once supple and stiff, gave him the air of a living bronze statue, so that a strange emptiness hung around him, as if he were not there. Every bronze statue was hollow and empty—but in his case that emptiness had a sucking attraction, like the center of a whirlpool. An indescribable sensation.

"All theater," said Julia, shrugging her shoulders. "In public he was always acting. Especially when he was in uniform."

"So perhaps you can say that Hitler was *playing* Hitler,"

ventured Herter, "like an actor plays a murderous Shake-spearean king, but in his case with real murders. When he goes into the wings between the acts, he changes into an unobtrusive man who lights up a cigarette."

Julia burst out laughing. "Hitler and a cigarette!"

"I'm not sure," said Falk. "Perhaps it's as you say. But that's not all. I've been thinking about him all my life, but there's always a last remaining bit that *I* can't explain even today, over half a century later. In two years' time, he will have been dead for as long as he lived." He had obviously taken the trouble to work this out. He shook his head. "For me he becomes more incomprehensible by the day."

Apart from that, the only figure Falk recognized in Hitler's entourage was the thickset figure of Bormann. Hitler's German shepherd Blondi raced joyfully down the steps and, yelping with joy, rested her front paws against his belt, whereupon he took her head in his gloved hand and gave it a brief kiss. At the top of the steps stood Miss Braun in an airy short-sleeved summer dress. . . .

"I knew," said Julia, interrupting him, "that she had stuffed a couple of handkerchiefs in her bra for the occasion."

A few yards behind her stood a group of officers from Hitler's personal SS bodyguard, in black, with white belts and right arms extended stiffly, hands in white gloves. He took off his hat, so that his strikingly pale forehead became visible, and gave her a gallant kiss on the hand; he greeted the others by loosely raising the palm of his right hand, as if preparing to carry a tray, after which he went inside via the gallery with Blondi, Braun, and her two Scottish terriers, Stasi and Negus. Eva's dearest wish, Julia knew, was a dachshund, but Hitler found dachshunds too stubborn and disobedient. He did not like those kinds of qualities.

"No one will ever understand," said Falk, his eyes downcast, while he slowly shook his head. "It was very unnerving. Every movement showed perfect control and precision, like with an acrobat, a trapeze artist. Of course he was a human being like everyone else, but at the same time he wasn't, more something like a work of art, a . . ." He shook his head. "I can't put it into words. Something horrible."

"You can put it into words very well," said Herter. "I myself have only to see him on film or in a photo, if necessary just his back, and I remember. He can't be explained with psychology; you need theology instead. It has an expression that may be applicable to him: *mysterium tremendum ac fascinans:* 'the at once horrific and fascinating secret.'"

Falk looked up in surprise. "Yes, it was something like that."

"Of course it isn't an explanation—the secret remains a secret—but perhaps it says something about the nature of the secret. That is, that he was actually nobody. A hollow statue, as you say. And the fascination he exerted and exerts to this day, and the power given him by the German people, was not *despite* the fact of his being soulless, but *because of* that fact." Herter sighed. "We must of course be careful that we don't deify him, even if it is with a negative sign. But if that one God (as history seems to indicate) does not exist, Hitler's deification perhaps touches the heart of the matter. In that case he is the deification of something that doesn't exist."

From one moment to the next, Herter's thoughts stumbled over each other like a pack of wolves in pursuit of a prey they have lost sight of. He would have preferred to make a few quick notes, but he was frightened that this would intimidate Falk. He heard Julia say something, but it did not get through to him. All inspired thinking happens in the blink of an eye, a flash from a threatening sky; only its thunderous development takes time. Shortly, today, he must take the time to record what he suddenly knew and at the same time did not know.

Because if all that were true, it might have a paradoxical consequence. If Hitler were the adored and cursed personification of nothingness, in whom there was nothing to restrain him from anything at all, his true face could not be revealed in a literary mirror, as Herter had suggested yesterday to Constant Ernst, since there *was* no face. In that case he was more comparable with Count Dracula, a vampire feeding on human blood: one of the "undead," with no reflection. Hence he was different not in degree but in essence from other despots, like Nero, Napoleon, or Stalin. They were demonic figures, but even demons are still something positive, whereas Hitler's essence was its absence. In a paradoxical way, precisely the *lack* of a "true face" was his true nature. Did that imply that Herter himself would have succeeded only if he did *not* manage to write his revelatory phantasm? In that case Hitler would have escaped for the umpteenth time, but he wouldn't get the chance this time.

Herter was alarmed at himself. Into what regions was he venturing? Wasn't he overstepping the mark? Danger was threatening. He must not shrink back. He had the feeling it was now or never; whatever must be, must be. If anyone on earth was qualified, it was himself. "Perhaps that's why I'm on earth," he had said to Maria yesterday—as if he, too, were an envoy from the Total Other.

But it seemed advisable to play it safe and insert a narrator between himself and his explosive story, as an insulator—a young man of about thirty-three, for whom the Second World War was further away than the First was for himself and who did *not* shrink from deifying Hitler, even if in some way he should become the victim of that. That would be his literary son—and his obvious first name was Otto: the product of the chemical reaction between "Rudolf Herter" and "Rudolf Otto," the theologian from whom the term *mysterium tremendum ac fascinans* derived. In any case he would not let himself be held back by anything else. It was precisely to that nihilistic divinity that Hitler must be nailed at the end of the twentieth century—after that Herter would not waste another word on him.

TEN

"You look pale," said Julia. "Are you feeling well?"

Herter looked up. "Not a hundred percent, to tell the truth. That's quite common at our age."

"Our? You're still a young man."

He took her wrinkled hand and pressed a kiss on it in traditional Austrian style. "Right," he said to Falk, "so he went in—and then?"

After three-quarters of an hour, there was a call to the kitchen, obviously from Miss Braun. Accompanied by Krause, he went upstairs, his heart pounding, dressed in his black trousers and white vest with the gold epaulets and the SS runes on its lapel against a black diamond-shaped background, in his white-gloved hands a tray of tea and biscuits. The Hitler that he found there, in his low-beamed study with a tiled stove taller than a man, was suddenly a completely different character. Drained, amorphous, in a gray double-breasted civilian suit, with socks down around his ankles, his hair still wet from the bath, he was flopped in a flower-patterned armchair, no more than the shadow of the demonic acrobat who had arrived

79

a short while ago—and totally unlike the rabble-rousing demagogue that the world knew. He was prodding his teeth with a toothpick.

"Obviously he was a kind of Unholy Trinity," said Herter.

Miss Braun was sitting on the sofa with her legs pulled up, under the portrait of Hitler's mother, long since dead, whom he closely resembled: the same Medusa look, the same small mouth. But he was not so exhausted that he had not immediately seen that Falk was new. While Krause, the heels of his boots together, introduced him with a few brief remarks, Hitler fixed him with his slightly bulging, dark blue eyes—and that look, said Falk, he would never forget.

"I think," said Herter, "that with that famous look he was deliberately forcing you into complete subjugation. You represented a potential danger for him; you were in a position where you could poison him. But with that look, which you would never forget, he paralyzed you like a snake does a rabbit."

As he suggested this, a phrase occurred to him that Thomas Mann had once used to characterize Hitler's look: his "basilisk stare." The basilisk, a winged creature of fable, consisting of a cockerel's head with the body of a serpent, incinerates everything it looks at, and even stones shatter at its stare. The only way in which it can be killed is to hold up a mirror to it, so that its all-destroying look is reflected back on itself, which constitutes a forced suicide. But even a basilisk is something positive, which can be reflected, while Hitler was pure negativity. Whoever looked in his eyes, experienced *horror vacui*.

"If only I'd done it," said Falk.

"If only you'd done *what*?"

"Poisoned him. But when I had reason to, it was no longer possible."

Herter nodded in silence. It was clear that Falk was now getting to what was really on his mind, but he did not want to harass him by asking about it. Falk was ridding himself of something that he and Julia had carried around with them for over half a century, and they must be given time. Herter forced himself not to show his impatience by looking at his watch, since however furtively one did so, it never went unnoticed. The solution was to look at someone else's watch, but neither Falk nor Julia was wearing one. He estimated that it was close to twelve.

Whenever the Chief fled the Wilhelmstrasse in hectic Berlin and with his arrival turned his country residence into his headquarters, other party high-ups would descend on the Obersalzberg with their families. There was Martin Bormann, of course, who lived in a large chalet in the inner circle of buildings and never lost sight of his master: he had had it built in such a way that from his balcony he could check with a telescope who came and went from Hitler's quarters. Marshal Göring had a house there, as did Albert Speer, Hitler's personal architect.

"With Speer he had his youthful Viennese dream within reach," Herter said, nodding.

"His youthful dream?"

"Of becoming an architect."

"Architect . . ." repeated Julia sarcastically. "Demolition man more like it. Because of him the whole of Germany was reduced to ash and rubble, and not only Germany."

Life on the mountain had something strangely dead about it, Falk continued, particularly when the Chief was there. Because he always stayed up late, like the true bohemian he had always remained at heart, he could not be woken before eleven. Afterward, in the war, that had cost the lives of thousands of his soldiers. If a report came in at eight o'clock that there had been a Russian offensive on the eastern front and a quick decision had to be taken whether to withdraw or counterattack, no one dared wake him, not even Field Marshal Keitel. The Führer was asleep! Generals were at their wits' end in Russia, but the Führer was asleep and must not be woken.

Yes, yes, yes, thought Herter. And what did he dream about? He would give a lot to know that.

"Did he ever tell you a dream, Mr. Falk?"

Falk laughed a short laugh.

"Did you think he ever let anyone get close? That man was shut up in himself . . . like . . . like . . . But once, in the war, in the winter of 1942, I think, he must have had a nightmare. I was woken by the sound of his screams. I grabbed my revolver and ran to his bedroom."

"You had a revolver?"

Falk looked up at him. "There were lots of weapons on the Obersalzberg, Mr. Herter. He was alone; Miss Braun was staying with relatives in Munich for a few days. Two of his SS bodyguards were already at the door with submachine guns, but they did not dare enter, even though someone might be murdering him. They were transferred to the eastern front the next day. I tore the door open and saw him standing bewildered in the middle of the room in his nightshirt, pouring with sweat; he looked at me with blue lips, his hair disheveled, his face contorted with fear. I shall never forget what he said: 'He . . . he . . . he . . . was here. . . .'"

He? Herter raised his eyebrows. He, of whom everyone was afraid—whom could he have been afraid of himself? Who was that "he"? His father? Wagner? The devil?

"But how could you have heard his screams? Didn't you say that you lived in an apartment building on the grounds?"

Falk exchanged a glance with Julia. "Not by this time."

Hitler's ascetic bedroom had no door to the corridor, only to his study. At eleven o'clock Falk would lay the morning papers and some telegrams on a chair there and call, "Good morning, my Führer! Time to get up!" The Chief would then usually appear in a long white nightshirt and slippers, but one time he had Falk come in. He was sitting on the edge of his bed, Miss Braun in a blue silk nightie on the floor; she was holding his foot in her lap and cutting his nails. Falk was struck by the whiteness of that foot.

"He was as white as that all over his body," added Julia. "Before the war I once saw him naked. It must have been in 1938—"

"No," Falk interrupted her, "in 1937."

She stared at him for a moment and obviously suddenly understood what he was driving at.

"Yes, of course. In 1937."

The Chief, he said, almost always stayed up far into the night, sometimes even till six or seven in the morning, surrounded by his usual clique: Bormann, Speer, his personal physician, his secretaries, his photographer, his chauffeur, his masseur, his young female vegetarian cook, a couple of orderlies, and other such staff, never the elite of his party, his armed forces, or his state.

"In that, too, he remained the Viennese bohemian," said Herter. "What are we supposed to make of the man?"

Julia herself was often allowed to join them. While Ullrich provided drinks and snacks, they would watch a film in the main reception room with huge tapestries, Arno Breker's gigantic bust of Wagner, and the largest window in the world, of which Hitler was so proud. Quite often it was a film banned by Goebbels. They also played records, Wagner of course, but also operettas like Franz Lehár's *Merry Widow*, after which the Chief would embark on one of his endless monologues, stretching from the distant past to the distant future, while his guests could scarcely keep their eyes open, partly because they had heard it all before. Afterward he would pace his study for hours, while in the summer he would often sit on the balcony of his study till sunrise, thinking in the silence of the mountains and the stars.

"Or so as not to have to sleep," said Herter, "because then he might have to deal with *him* again. Anyway, it doesn't bear thinking about, what he brooded on, on that balcony."

"That's true," said Falk. "It's just as well that after the war that haunted castle, or what was left of it after the American bombing, was razed to the ground."

But Miss Braun, continued Julia, withdrew to her room at about one o'clock, where Julia brought her a mug of hot chocolate. That night she knocked, but because Blondi was barking in Hitler's study to gain the attention of her orating master, she did not hear whether Miss Braun had said "Come in" as always. She opened the door and saw them standing in the middle of the room, in an intimate embrace, she with her nightie hanging open, a black one this time, he with nothing on. His fleshy white body had something dead about it—it had never seen the sun—only his cheeks and neck had some color, but that stopped abruptly, so that it was as if his head came from another body. Julia could still remember that the door to the bathroom was open and that steam and the sound of splashing water was coming out. She could not see what they were doing, but he was standing with his back to the door and was obviously in a state of arousal. "Patscherl . . ." she heard him groan.

"Patscherl?" repeated Herter.

"He had lots of those affectionate names for her," said Julia. "Feferl, for example."

"Tschapperl," added Falk with a deadpan expression. "Schnacksi."

Miss Braun looked at her over his shoulder and opened her eyes wide in alarm, whereupon Julia closed the door quickly and silently. Thank God he had not noticed anything.

"Things could have gone badly wrong," said Falk. "If they had been standing ninety degrees from where they were, that could have cost us our lives within ten minutes." He dabbed his eyes with a handkerchief, but that had nothing to do with emotion, only old age.

Now there was a knock at the door, and, without waiting for an answer, a small, bearded man in a brown duster coat appeared. After a quick look into the room, he asked, with a smile that Herter did not like at all, "A visitor?"

"As you can see," said Falk without looking at him.

The man waited for a moment for a fuller explanation; when none was forthcoming, he took a rubbish bag from the kitchen cupboard and disappeared without a word.

A silence fell that Herter deliberately did not break. For most people alive today, Hitler had by now become just a figure from violent films or farces, but here Julia and Ullrich Falk were up to their necks in memories of that submerged time. They had been on the spot, for them it was all yesterday, and they could go on talking endlessly about him, if only to put off what they really wanted to say. When the silence began to become embarrassing, what he had hoped for happened. The two exchanged a look, after which Falk got up and checked to see that no one was listening at the door.

He sat down again and said, "One day in May 1938, shortly after the annexation of Austria, we learned there were to be guests; with Mrs. Mittlstrasser, the wife of the head of domestic services, we were laying the table for lunch. That always had to be done carefully, as the Chief sometimes knelt down on one knee to check with one eye that all the glasses were in line."

"That was his architect's eye," observed Herter. "That's how he looked at Speer's models of Germania and at his troops on parade."

"Suddenly Linge appeared in the dining room and told us that the Führer wished to speak to us."

"Linge?" asked Herter.

"He was the successor of Krause."

"We were terrified," said Julia. "If he wanted anything from us, he always phoned himself; we were never officially summoned."

Upstairs, in his study, where he had forced whole countries to their knees with shouting and threats, a select company was sitting on the wide sofa and in the armchairs: the Chief and Miss Braun, Bormann, the massive majordomo Brückner, and the head of domestic services, also an officer. The two of them stood there intimidated; there was a tension in the room, but Brückner instructed Linge to fetch two chairs from the library. That was reassuring at least, but it made the situation all the more incomprehensible. What business had they, two humble domestic servants in their twenties, with all these bigwigs?

When they were seated, on upright peasant chairs, Linge received a brief look from Brückner indicating that he should disappear instantly.

With his elegant hand resting on the neck of Blondi, who sat next to his armchair with her ears pricked like a proud creature from another, more innocent world, Hitler said that this was undoubtedly the most important day in their lives, since he had decided to place a responsibility of world-historical significance on their shoulders. He paused and glanced at the Lady Chief, who was sitting palely between the two officers Brückner and Mittlstrasser on the sofa.

"Mr. Falk, Mrs. Falk," said Hitler formally, "I'm going to disclose a state secret to you: Miss Braun is expecting a child."

ELEVEN

"No!" cried Herter. "It's not true!"

Was this possible? In astonishment he tried to take it in. Had these two ancient people in this old-people's home really heard those words over sixty years ago from that mouth below the square mustache? Perhaps it was not of world-historical significance, but it was certainly earth-shattering. Hitler—a child! It was the last thing Herter could have dreamed up himself—but obviously that was how reality worked: it was always one step ahead of the imagination. He would have most liked to know the rest of the story in ten sentences. Where was the child? Was it still alive? But his instinct told him that he must let them find their own tempo; they were old, and everything was slower then, including the telling of a story.

"We were just as shocked as you," said Julia. "We did not understand a thing. The fact that Miss Braun was pregnant by the Chief was in itself nothing special. These things simply happen, even in royal circles, perhaps especially there. Anyway, it had struck me that in the last few weeks she was constantly craving herring and gherkins. But what was all that to do with us? What kind of responsibility was being put on our shoulders?"

That was then explained to them by Bormann. The problem was, he said, that all German women wanted a child by the Führer. They called their sons Adolf anyway. If he were now to marry Miss Braun, and if it were subsequently to emerge that he had become the father of a child, supposedly born two months premature, they would feel that he had betrayed them, and that was undesirable for political reasons—after all, it was mainly women who had brought him to power. Brückner burst out laughing and said that the head of Chancellery certainly always knew how to present things succinctly. Miss Braun was obviously irritated, but even the Chief had to laugh briefly, and his eyes rolled completely backward for a moment as if they were looking inside, into the darkness of his skull.

"And what did your responsibility consist of?" asked Herter, still not recovered from his astonishment.

"That it must appear to be our child," said Falk.

Herter sighed. He could forget his own story now, including his literary son Otto, but he no longer cared. All he wanted to do was listen to theirs.

That morning the Chief took no further interest in the matter. Apathetic, as if it did not concern him, he tucked in to the biscuits with drooping shoulders and looked out the window at the wild, awesome rocky massif of the Untersberg, gray as cigarette ash above the tree line, with occasional patches of snow. According to a South German legend, the Hohenstaufen emperor, Friederich I, otherwise known as Barbarossa, was asleep inside the Untersberg; one day he would open his eyes and, after crushing the Jewish Antichrist, would found the

Thousand-Year Empire, leaving the plain of Salzburg ankle deep in blood. Probably Hitler had already thought up the code name for his invasion of the Soviet Union three years later: *Operation Barbarossa*.

The scenario that Hitler and his intimates turned out to have devised was acted out step-by-step in the following months and years. First of all, that very week, Ullrich and Julia had to move to the Berghof itself. Two guest rooms on the same corridor onto which the rooms of the Chief and the Lady Chief also gave, up to then reserved exclusively for personal guests such as the family of the Lady Chief, were cleared and fitted out for them. One could give as a reason that the Führer and Miss Braun wished to have their personal servants closer to them. For the rest of the war, Falk was given exemption from military service. They must also quickly write home and say that they were expecting a child, then submit the letters to Bormann, just as he would check all their outgoing mail from then on. Moreover, Bormann gave them to understand that they must put out of their heads the idea of having children of their own—that would be considered as insubordination. The obvious thing would have been to charge Hitler's personal physician, Dr. Morell, formerly a fashionable doctor on the Kurfürstendamm specializing in high-society venereal diseases, with the care of Miss Braun, but that would have aroused suspicion; the other members of the staff relied on the SS garrison doctor, but he was too close to things. Therefore it was decided to involve the GP of Berchtesgaden, Dr. Krüger, an elderly, distinguished gentleman with a well-groomed white mustache and bow tie, who thus acquired a certain Mrs. Falk as a patient. He was sworn in and intimidated in covert terms by

Bormann personally. Miss Braun was happy with that course of events, as she did not like a doctor in uniform, and maintained that Morell had an unpleasant body odor.

After that, time was left to do its work. Four months later, when Miss Braun's bulge could no longer be unobtrusively concealed with clothing, the second phase began. One afternoon, when the Chief was in Berlin, a car drew up with an unknown driver, who loaded her empty cases while she said good-bye to the secretaries and Julia, ostensibly bound for Italy on an extended art tour. Not even the secretaries believed that ruse—it was obviously over between her and the Führer, but no one dared mention it. There were tears, but Miss Braun kept her composure. For the driver, a Gestapo man who had learned not to ask any questions, she was a certain Miss Wolf; he drove to Linz, where they had a meal in the Rathskeller, and in the middle of the night they returned to the Berghof, without being stopped at any of the countless sentry posts. Julia had heard all this from Miss Braun herself.

Herter had to force himself not to listen openmouthed; he had not been so under the spell of a story since his childhood. But it wasn't a story—that is, it was not made up, as children say; it had "really happened," since it was inconceivable that those two ancient people here in Eben Haëzer could make up something like this.

Until her confinement in November, Miss Braun could now no longer leave the Führer's wing. She must not show herself at the windows, and at night no light must be seen in her room. Only the conspirators still had access to her, and from then Julia's role was to play the part of a pregnant woman. Every morning she went to the mirror with Miss Braun and stuffed all kinds of cloths, towels, and later cushions under her clothes so as to represent faithfully the growth of the Führer's child. That was accompanied by a lot of fun, and Miss Braun always wanted to know exactly how they had reacted down-stairs to Julia's pregnancy. Hitler particularly enjoyed inquiring in company how she was feeling. He was also in the habit of sending her to bed early in the evenings, because of her condition.

"Of course I had to be careful," said Falk, "that my wife did not really become pregnant. That would have sabotaged the whole plan, and Bormann would have destroyed us. It used to be more difficult than it is now—not destruction, I mean, but not getting pregnant."

"I know all about it," sighed Herter. "I went through it all myself. And how did Miss Braun pass her days during those months in her room?"

Since she must of course have something to talk about in November and should preferably not say that she had drunk coffee on the Piazza San Marco in Florence and visited the Uffizi in Rome, she was provided by the father-to-be with Baedekers, art books, and the standard works of Burckhardt, *The Civilization of the Renaissance in Italy* and *Cicerone*. With Blondi at her feet, she studied daily—usually at Hitler's massive oak desk when he was not there. In order to give her support, he was there often during those months; that was why, during his preparations for the invasion of Czechoslovakia, he had had Chamberlain come not to Berlin but to the Berghof. Next to her bed lay Goethe's *Italian Journey*. She spent all day in her nightie; Julia washed her underwear in the bath. Because Julia, pregnant as she was, preferred to eat quietly in her room but seemed to have a huge appetite, Falk always took a triple portion upstairs. Mittlstrasser now also had one of the Falks' rooms fitted out as a nursery, including a traditional German cradle with Bavarian carving.

"Finally," said Julia, after lighting up yet another cigarette, "I had the feeling that I was expecting any day. Eventually I had to take things easier, as Dr. Krüger had said to 'Mrs. Falk,' since I was supposedly getting tired more easily, and I remember even feeling involuntarily rather offended when he came for a checkup and of course did not see me."

Whenever Krüger pulled up at the Berghof in his puttering, two-stroke DKW that seemed to be made of papier-mâché, he brought with him an atmosphere of civilization. Then, in the afternoon of November 9, labor began. All day long there was a restless feeling in the house; there were obviously some political goings-on. Downstairs in the large reception room, where a number of functionaries were gathered, all in uniform, Hitler sat telephoning nonstop, to Göring and Himmler in Berlin. Falk knew that because he called them by their surnames; the only one he had ever been on first-name terms with seemed to have been Röhm, the leader of the SA, but Hitler had had him executed a few years earlier. Bormann was also there, of course. Meanwhile Miss Braun was taken to the Falks' quarters, where she was to give birth, since the cries of mother and child must come from the right direction. In addition an SS ambulance had been stationed next to the Berghof, in case there should be a problem and Mrs. Falk had to be brought to a hospital in Salzburg. Julia had taken off the cloths and cushions and helped with the birth, which took place at about midnight.

"And?" asked Herter.

"A boy," said Julia. She glanced at the photo on the television, and there were tears in her eyes.

Herter looked questioningly at Falk, who nodded.

"That was already during the war. Miss Braun took that photo."

"Do you mind?"

Herter got up and studied the photo more closely. The little boy was standing feet apart and confident on a terrace in a white blouse, white shorts, and white knee-length stockings, taking a bite from a sandwich. The look in his eyes did indeed seem to have something of the piercing quality that characterized his father. His father? Was this really Hitler's son? The thought still struck Herter as totally absurd, but why, actually?

"There was sugar on that sandwich," said Julia. "I made it myself. That's me, next to him."

Now he knew, he could see. The slim young woman in her late twenties still shimmered through Julia, like a figure behind frosted glass, though conversely there was no hint of the fat, ancient lady that she would become. Herter turned around.

"What was his name?"

"Siegfried," said Falk with a sigh, which at the same time seemed a sigh of relief at having finally unburdened himself of his lifelong secret.

"Of course," said Herter, raising his hand briefly before sitting down again. "Siegfried. I might have known. The great Germanic hero who knew no fear. That's what Wagner called his son, too. And how did the Chief react to the birth of his son?"

Majordomo Brückner had given him the news downstairs, Falk told him, and when he came pale-faced into the room, with Bormann hard on his heels, and saw his Patscherl lying there with his child at her breast, it was as if what was happening scarcely sank in. Hitler's thoughts were somewhere completely different—namely, on his first pogrom, which he had ordered that same night. As they heard the following day, the synagogues burned everywhere in Germany and Austria, and the windows of Jewish shops were smashed. "The Night of Broken Glass," it was later called—and it was the same November 9 on which the German emperor had been deposed in 1918, on which Hitler's coup had failed in Munich in 1923, and on which in 1989 the Berlin Wall had fallen.

"So the final end of his action and its consequences," said Herter, "came sixty-six years after the beginning. Almost the Number of the Beast. Exactly a hundred years after his birth." In a sinister way, everything always added up with Hitler.

But the Chief soon recovered and looked as if he had suddenly forgotten his pogrom. Miss Braun was overjoyed that she had not borne him a daughter, and after he had given the mother a stiff kiss on the hand, Julia laid the baby carefully in his arms. He looked terribly awkward, pressed Siegfried against the Iron Cross on his chest, gazed around in a kind of clumsy ecstasy, and said solemnly, "A child is born."

Mittlstrasser whispered respectfully that this was a quotation from an opera by Wagner. Only Bormann seemed somehow none too happy at the arrival of the child; he looked as if he would prefer to ask it for its papers.

Then a precarious period began. Ullrich drove with Mittlstrasser to the Registry Office in Berchtesgaden to register the child: *Siegfried Falk* instead of *Siegfried Braun*. In the next few days, Julia received visits from the secretaries and other members of the staff in the bed in which she had given birth, while her room turned into a florist's shop. Her parents were allowed to come to the Berghof. That, said Julia, had been the most difficult moment of the whole comedy for her: when her mother took her supposed grandchild in her arms with tears of happiness. Her father, on the other hand, who was in SS uniform, seemed more fascinated by the Holy of Holies in which he found himself than by his grandson.

After a week the supposed Mrs. Falk was allowed by Dr. Krüger to start work again carefully. Miss Braun, who was secretly breast-feeding her child, also returned around that time. Weak and exhausted from her extensive journey—in the dead of night, as she said, and in a certain sense that was not a lie. After each feed she had Julia bind the large breasts she had suddenly developed with a silk shawl; in addition she wore wide woolen sweaters, as it was cold at the Berghof after Sicily, where she had recently climbed Vesuvius. Falk told him that, during the welcome-home lunch, Speer had repeated in amazement, "Vesuvius? In Sicily? Of course you mean Etna?" Of course, Miss Braun had said, blushing—Vesuvius, Etna . . . she always got them mixed up. Whereupon the Chief said, between two mouthfuls of his pseudosteak made of vegetables, that in a certain sense those two volcanoes were manifestations of one and the same primeval volcano, like himself and Napoleon.

TWELVE

There was another knock, but this time the visitor waited until Julia had called "Come in." A thickset woman in her forties, with calves like upturned champagne bottles, appeared in the room.

"Mr. Herter," said Falk, introducing him, "Mrs. Brandstätter. Mrs. Brandstätter is our director."

Herter got up and put out his hand, whereupon she stared at him in astonishment for a few seconds, as if he were the last person she expected.

"Didn't I see you on television last night?"

It was immediately clear to Herter that he must think up an explanation on the spot for his presence. What was a famous foreign writer, who actually appeared on television, doing in the apartment of this poor old couple in her old-people's home in an out-of-the-way corner of Vienna? She suspected something; probably she knew whom she had in her home— although she did not know what he now knew—and wanted to protect them.

"Just like Mr. and Mrs. Falk. We're going over old memo-

99

ries. Mr. and Mrs. Falk went to my reading to see if I were the same person as the young writer they once met by chance forty years ago."

"And?" asked the director, looking from one to the other.

"I never change," said Herter, with something resembling a smile.

She said that she did not wish to interrupt them any further, and, without saying why she had actually come, took her leave.

"Should Mrs. Brandstätter ask any more about our meeting," said Herter after her departure, "you must think up something for yourself. I don't know what your circumstances were forty years ago."

"They were very reasonable again by then," said Falk, "after having been less reasonable for a while. After the war we spent two years in an American internment camp."

Julia got up, stubbed out her cigarette and asked, "Would you like a sandwich perhaps? I'm ashamed that we've kept you so long."

Herter looked at his watch: a quarter to one. Perhaps he should give Maria a ring, but it did not seem sensible to shatter the intimacy.

"I'd love a sandwich, and it would be odd if I were to say I must be getting along, when I hear that Hitler had a son. Do the two of you actually realize how sensational what you've told me is? If you had offered it to *Der Spiegel* and ten other such magazines worldwide, you would have earned millions. You wouldn't have lived in this flat in Eben Haëzer, but in a villa as big as the Berghof, with your own staff."

Falk's eyes suddenly took on a cool look.

"For the time being that also applies to you. You swore an oath just now."

With a feeling of shame that was not entirely feigned, Herter bowed his head for a moment. Falk had put him in his place. Anyway, who would believe him? And after the death of the Falks, without witnesses, he would be even less credible. He would be praised for his imagination, and perhaps be awarded a literary prize for it, but no one would believe him.

"Apart from which," said Falk, "you haven't yet heard the half of it."

In the kitchen Julia pressed a large, round, dark brown loaf to her chest and with a long knife cut off thin slices in a way that made him shiver. Nowhere in the world did bread have its throat cut like this. He was also given a glass of beer, and as he sank his teeth into the slice, spread with goose fat and horseradish and liberally sprinkled with salt, he was again overcome by the feeling of roots that he had only in Austria. It tasted better than a priceless lunch in a three-star restaurant in Riquewihr.

"And then?" he asked: the central question of all narrative.

Then the happiest time of their lives began.

Of course they were watched more closely than before, and family visits from Vienna were no longer possible. Every six months the deceived grandparents were allowed to appear at the Berghof for an afternoon, when Julia's father was always disappointed at not seeing the Führer. What it came down to was that they were prisoners, but their little Siggi, who wasn't their Siggi, made up for everything. For the first three years, when he conquered ten countries, the Chief was more at the Berghof than in Berlin. He received kings and presidents there, whom he threatened and swore at, so loudly that it could be heard even in the kitchen, after which they were offered a meal by a suddenly utterly charming Führer and went to their cars still trembling with fear past the SS guard of honor, in the awareness that their country was doomed. To the sorrow of Miss Braun, her fiancé was not very interested in his little son to begin with. He might be the all-powerful Führer, who had his eye on world domination, but he was obviously not cut out to be a father: for that he was too much of a mommy's boy himself. Besides, the child was probably as yet too small and interchangeable with other babies and toddlers.

He once said to Falk that the boy would very probably never amount to anything, since great men always had insignificant sons: you could see that from August, Goethe's son. But in this case his insignificance would be laid at Falk's door. The fact that Siegfried existed at all he owed to the entreaties of Miss Braun, whom he had to leave alone so often because of his busy activities in the service of the German people. He forbade Falk to pass on his remark to Miss Braun, but Julia was just as shocked by it as Miss Braun would have been. As the years went by, in fact, she had a stronger and stronger feeling that the child was really hers, since it was treated as such by everyone, in public even by the seven initiates. When he was allowed to attend the nursery school run by Mrs. Podlech, which Bormann had set up at the Berghof for his own children, those of Speer, and those of a few other highly placed officials, such as Göring's little daughter, she was certainly prouder than the real mother. It was never mentioned, but perhaps Miss Braun struggled with the same feeling of jealousy. If Siggi was in pain or unhappy, he cried not on her shoulder but on Julia's; if he had had a nightmare, he crawled into Julia's bed, not his mother's.

Oh, those marvelous, dazzling winter days of 1941 and 1942 in the deep, deep snow, at the windows the transparent fangs of the icicles, and those jolly New Year's Eves with the "lead casting," which Dr. Goebbels once attended. Did they have that tradition in Holland?

"No," said Herter, "but in my home we did."

There was a hunt in the attic for some piece of lead piping, which was put on the gas in an old saucepan. He could still see the gray skin on the molten lead and his father handing him the tin spoon with which he must scoop up some of it and let it slip into a dish of water. The shape that then emerged with much hissing was fished out and commented upon by everyone, because it foretold the future. Falk half turned around and rummaged a bit in a drawer. He took out a shiny rectangular object, no larger than a little finger, which he handed to Herter.

"This is Hitler's. I kept it. What do you think? I still remember that he was unhappy about it."

Herter looked in fascination at the odd shape. Of course he knew that it had been created by the laws of chance—that is, determined by the height of the spoon above the water and the speed at which the lead had been poured in, and that it could just as well have been someone else's. But at the same time he knew that it was no one else's but Hitler's. He had made it and he had not made it. It reminded him vaguely of a basilisk, like the one Thomas Mann had written about—but he was not sure that he would not also have thought this if he had heard that the thing derived from Gandhi. For some reason the look of the metal reminded him of Hitler's deathly pale forehead.

As he was about to give it back without comment, Falk said, "I'm giving it to you as a present."

Herter nodded and put it silently into the breast pocket of his shirt. Something prevented him from thanking Falk.

And then those long summer afternoons on the big terrace above the garage or in the swimming pool at Göring's villa . . .

There were also occasional trips by Miss Braun to her family in Munich or to see a girlfriend in Italy, on which she could not go without Julia, who in turn could not leave her son alone; in the front seat sat the driver and a Gestapo man, while in the back the three of them played games. Siggi grew into a hyperactive little boy, who could not hold his tongue or sit still for a second. He gabbled on nonstop, even to Blondi and Miss Braun's dogs. If he did something, he would announce that he was doing it, at the same time letting himself fall back into an armchair, thumping the cushions, performing somersaults, standing on his head, and crawling along the floor like a little monster, all the while calling out to "Auntie Effi" or "Uncle Wolf" to make sure they could see what he was getting up to.

Uncle Wolf, repeated Herter in his thoughts. What was it with Hitler and wolves? Just the fact that they were beasts of prey, too? In the 1920s "Wolf" was his cover name; his later headquarters in East Prussia, Russia, and northern France were called "Wolf's Lair," "Wehrwolf," and "Wolf's Gorge." Blondi, too, looked like a wolf; he called one of the pups she produced toward the end of the war, and which he wanted to rear himself, "Wolfie." *Homo homini lupus*—man is a wolf to other men. Was there self-knowledge behind it?

In the summer of 1941, Operation Barbarossa had begun— but, said Falk, as far as he was concerned, it actually passed him by. He, too, had once begun at the very bottom as a political activist, with a revolver in his hand, but since big politics had been acted out before his eyes while he served coffee and cakes, he could no longer grasp it and lost his interest in it. Only after the war had he realized all that the Chief had been up to in those days—for example, what he talked to Himmler about on their long walks to the teahouse, with climbing sticks and sunglasses on, out of earshot of the entourage. Even Fegelein was never there.

"Fegelein?" repeated Herter. "Who was Fegelein?"

"SS General Hermann Fegelein," said Falk. "A charming young senior officer, Himmler's personal representative with Hitler. 'Himmler's eyes,' he was called. At Hitler's insistence he had married Miss Braun's sister Gretl. That was of course to give Miss Braun more prestige at court, as the sister-in-law of General Fegelein. Hitler gave a great party on their wedding, but Fegelein cared very little for Gretl."

"He went on chasing women," said Julia, with an expression that indicated that there were degrees of badness. "There were terrible scenes every time."

Behind the eastern front, Falk continued, thousands were already being murdered, and in the summer of 1942, the first trains started rolling through Europe to the extermination camps. He shook his head for a moment, as if he still could not believe what he was saying.

"Everything progressed as he had determined from the start. From day to day, his life's goal came closer: the complete destruction of Jewry, without any of us suspecting a thing. Miss Braun included."

"Looking back," said Julia, "we think that he was intoxicated with what he was doing. He was convinced that he would be considered for all eternity as the savior of mankind and the greatest figure in world history. As a result his relationship to his young son also changed."

It struck everyone that Hitler began to pay more attention to him, at least when there were no uninitiated people around. Falk had once seen him with Siggi on his arm in his study, telling him something and pointing outside, to the Untersberg. Or he had Siggi on his lap and drew a rustic Viennese cityscape for him, which he could do very well, since he had talent and a photographic memory; he would have his reading glasses on, the existence of which Germany must not know about. Another time—shortly after the devastating bombing of Hamburg in July 1943—he was kneeling on the ground and they were playing together with a Schuco that Hitler had given him: a toy car that you had to wind up and that could be steered via a wire from the roof. In order not to awaken suspicion, he could of course give him only very simple presents. And Julia once heard him say to Bormann on the terrace when Miss Braun was there, "Maybe I'll found a dynasty. Then I'll adopt Siegfried, just as Julius Caesar did with the later emperor Augustus."

He said it laughingly, but perhaps it was more than a joke after all. You could expect anything of him.

THIRTEEN

More and more frequently, Hitler withdrew for weeks or months on end to his headquarters in East Prussia. On the Russian front, the Jewish-Bolshevik subhumans had been advancing alarmingly since the Battle of Stalingrad, and in North Africa as well things were no longer going according to plan, so that Jerusalem, the Jewish objective of the campaign, unfortunately had to be written off; meanwhile Germany's cities were being turned to ruins one after another under the Anglo-American terror bombing, but no one on the staff wanted to face the situation, not even after the invasion of June 1944: as long as the Führer believed immutably in final victory, people need not worry about their august positions at court. The secret weapon, which according to Goebbels was being developed, would soon instantly change the odds in the war. In reality it was being forged in America, like the Wagnerian magic sword Nothung, under the direction of Jewish scientists exiled from Germany. Meanwhile, Herter was told, the system, under Bormann's management, was already beginning to burrow underground. For the past year, hundreds of foreign slave laborers had been working day and night to construct labyrinthine passages and bunkers under the whole Berghof site, which linked all the buildings. They were fully equipped, from the quarters of the Chief and Lady Chief with their paneling in precious wood to a kennel for Blondi, as well as kitchens, storerooms, nurseries, offices, archives, a headquarters, telex rooms, and a Gestapo control room, with machine-gun nests at strategic points and crowned aboveground by pillboxes with rapid-firing cannon.

Miss Braun, too, shut herself off from the reality of the war, which on the Obersalzberg manifested itself only in the form of muffled underground explosions. Occasionally there were air-raid warnings, which were obviously immediately reported to the Chief, because he invariably called a few minutes later to insist that Miss Braun go to the air-raid shelter.

She was sad when her Adi was away from home, but now she had her son, and Julia no longer had to put her lover's portrait by her plate. Still, it cannot have escaped even her that the oppressive feeling immediately lifted from the Berghof when the column of black Mercedeses with motorcycle escort had disappeared around the corner—taking everyone and everything with it—Bormann, Morell, Brückner's successor Schaub, Heinz Linge, the secretaries, the cook, Blondi, and twenty large trunks containing the Chief's luggage. Cigarettes were lit up, and suddenly there was occasional laughter to be heard, even from the quarters of the SS companies; from somewhere there even came the sound of an American jazz record on a portable gramophone, degenerate black music, that is, like the waters of a flooding river starting to seep through the dike. The other bigwigs also left the mountain, which overnight had become redundant. Julia could still remember Mrs. Speer once commenting to her as she said good-bye that Siggi was looking more and more like her. Miss Braun couldn't help laughing a little and pouting at the same time.

"In mid-July 1944—" said Falk, "Siggi was almost six by then—the Chief again left for his Wolf's Lair. Saying good-bye to Miss Braun and Siggi took a long time, as if he knew that he would never see the Berghof again. He had already turned into a stooping old man." Falk sat up a little and stared hard at Herter. After a brief hesitation, he said, "The following week Count Stauffenberg made his assassination attempt. Miss Braun was desperate because she could not support her lover and only had telephone contact with him, since he wanted her to stay with Siggi. He did, though, send her his torn and bloodstained uniform. And then, two months later, the catastrophe began for us."

Herter saw that Falk had suddenly made his decision, like someone who does not dare jump from a burning house into a safety net and then suddenly does so after all. Next to him he heard a suppressed sob from Julia but forced himself not to look to the side.

"I'm sorry, Mr. Herter, but what I am about to tell you is completely incomprehensible—not only for you but still for us, too. The Chief had not rung for a few days, and when Miss Braun tried to reach him, she was constantly told that he was too busy to come to the phone. This worried her, but what could she do? On Friday, September 22, a radiant autumn day—I shall never forget it—toward midday, Bormann suddenly appeared by the great steps, in a closed car, with a small entourage in a second vehicle. I found that strange in itself: in summer the gentlemen always drove with the hood down. And come to that, what could be the matter that made him willing to lose sight of his master for a few days? I had hung out the uniforms and suits of the Chief to air on the balcony, and I was polishing his boots and shoes—of course I did not know that he would never wear any of them again; he had an extensive wardrobe in Berlin and in his field headquarters, too. It had all been made to measure, and I knew how particular he was about his clothes. His uniforms, his jackets, his caps—he designed everything himself, just like his buildings, his flags, his standards, and his mass events. If there were so much as a small crease somewhere that he didn't like, he would send for Mr. Hugo, his tailor."

It was obvious that Falk was still trying to put off saying what he had to say. Herter nodded. "He was a perfectionist."

"Ullrich came immediately to tell us what was happening," said Julia. "I was in the library with Mrs. Köppe. That was also on the upper floor. We were dusting books at the open window, Miss Braun was reading aloud from the children's book *Shock-Headed Peter*, while Siggi was constantly standing on his head and letting himself fall full length on the divan. The library was the only place in the Berghof that was at all inviting. Now and then you could hear the dynamite thundering deep in the mountain."

Falk glanced at the smile that had appeared on Herter's face and which he of course did not understand—it was because Herter suddenly imagined *what* books were being knocked together at the window that day: Schopenhauer against Gobineau, Nietzsche against Karl May, Houston Stewart Chamberlain against Wagner . . .

"We looked at each other in alarm," said Falk, and it was as if that alarm seemed to appear in his eyes again after fifty years. "A little later, probably after he had spoken to Mittlstrasser, Bormann came upstairs. I don't know . . . from the stamping of his boots on the stairs I sensed that something was wrong. It was just a little too loud, as if he were trying to give himself courage. Stasi and Negus smelled a rat, too, and started barking.

"'My God,' said Mrs. Köppe, 'what can that mean?'

"When he came in, he clicked his heels, gave the German salute, and said formally 'Heil Hitler.' That was not the custom at the Berghof, and we simply mumbled something. Only Siggi looked at him wide-eyed. Bormann did not take off his cap and fixed his gaze on Mrs. Köppe, who took the hint and left the room. Then he said to Miss Braun that the Führer had expressed the wish to have her with him in these difficult days."

"A great weight fell from us," Julia added. "Mrs. Braun's face brightened completely. She asked when she was to go. Right away, said Bormann; the car was waiting outside to take her to the airport at Salzburg, where a plane was on the runway. 'And what about Siggi?' I can still hear her asking—of course Siggi was going, too, like Ullrich and me? No, said Bormann, the Führer had decided that he should stay at the Berghof with his legal parents. The Wolf's Lair was no environment for a child; apart from that it was too dangerous, so close to the front."

"Of course that put her in a quandary," said Falk, "but she also knew that there was no arguing with a decision of Hitler's. Bormann still had not moved. He said that she must immediately go and pack; he informed me curtly that we would be speaking shortly. Then he turned on his heel and marched out of the room."

The cases, which had already left the Berghof empty once, were now packed to capacity—mainly by Julia. She said that Miss Braun mostly sat on the edge of the bed with her arm around the shoulders of Siggi, who was meanwhile playing with a little compass. She had tears in her eyes and said that she would come and visit him very often. He had no idea why Auntie Effi was so terribly sad, since wasn't she going to see Uncle Wolf, who was waging war? He had once told the Chief that when he was grown up, he wanted to wage war, too. The Chief had laughed till he cried.

Miss Braun phoned her family in Munich, since in the Wolf's Lair they would not be able to reach her. A little later everyone was lined up in the hall—including Mrs. Bormann and her children, whom Bormann always left at the Obersalzberg, so that he could chase the girls at headquarters unhindered. The farewells were formal. She shook hands with Julia and Ullrich, gave Siggi a kiss on the forehead and the terriers a kiss, too, and got into the second car, which had a Gestapo man sitting next to the driver.

"An hour later," said Falk, "an adjutant of Bormann's appeared and said that the head of Chancellery was expecting me in his chalet."

"I don't know why," said Julia, "but for some reason I felt at once that there was something else in the air. I took Siggi to his room, where the floor was covered with his toy soldiers, who were positioned as if carrying out an offensive. I remember he said that it was a nuisance that he had only German soldiers; you ought to have Russian soldiers, too, so that you could win, but you couldn't buy them. Like this, without an enemy, you couldn't even lose."

Herter was reminded of Marnix. Marnix, too, could have said something like that, but he no longer played with stationary soldiers; he played computer games in which a visible enemy could be destroyed. Herter himself, eleven years older than Siegfried Falk, alias Braun, alias Hitler, had played with toy soldiers before the war, also in German uniforms, without ever having missed an opposing army. Obviously he had been concerned not with depicting the battle but with creating impressive tableaux, not as a general but as a director. Perhaps Hitler, the man of the theater who regarded himself as the greatest commander of all time, had only played theatrically with toy soldiers, albeit of flesh and blood.

It was five minutes' walk to Bormann's chalet, which was somewhat smaller than the Berghof but larger than Göring's. The sun shone on the slope that Falk climbed up, gardeners were mowing the grass, birds were singing in the trees—everything would have been idyllic but for the muffled thud of pneumatic hammers everywhere under the ground. He, too, was not wholly at ease, but what could be up? No one had done anything wrong. When his colleague let him in, he heard somewhere in the depths of the house the laughter and twittering of Bormann's children. The head of Chancellery received him standing in his study, feet slightly apart, hands on hips. "Falk," he had said, "we can be brief. Prepare yourself."

For a moment Falk was unable to continue. He seemed to become even smaller; he bent his head, rubbed his face with both hands, and said in a choking voice, "He said, 'On the Führer's orders, you are to kill Siegfried.'"

FOURTEEN

Herter's mouth fell open. Where was he? This could not be true! Beside him he could hear Julia sobbing into her handkerchief. So had it happened after all? It just wasn't thinkable! And why, why did it have to happen? When he saw Falk looking at Julia, he got up and with a gesture suggested changing places. On the sofa Falk put his hand on Julia's, and, sitting opposite, he felt Falk's warmth in the small armchair.

"I can't believe my ears," Herter said. "You had to *kill* Siegfried? Hitler's son, Siggi, whom he doted on? Why, in heaven's name?"

"I still don't know to this day," said Falk. "I felt as if I was turning into a pillar of ice. When I could speak again, I of course also asked that question, but Bormann snapped, 'An order is not explained, Falk, but given. The Führer is the last person to be accountable to you.' I realized it was pointless to discuss it further. The Chief had taken his unfathomable decision, and so it must happen. You should know that in those days an order from the Führer had in the most literal sense the force of law. I summoned up courage to ask what the consequences would be if I refused."

"And?" asked Herter, when Falk remained silent.

"In that case Siegfried would die anyway, as he had been sentenced to death. That was irrevocable. The Führer never went back on a decision. But in addition Julia and I would be sent to a concentration camp, and perhaps I could imagine something of what that would mean. If I loved my wife, he said, it might be more sensible not to refuse."

"And Miss Braun? Did Miss Braun know about it?"

"I don't know, Mr. Herter. I know no more than I'm telling you."

"I'm speechless," said Herter. "What kind of creatures were they? They were what they said the Jews were: vermin out for world domination. What scum! But actually we knew that anyway."

"Yes, you say that now, but at the time I didn't really know. For the first time in all those years, it dawned on me with a jolt the kind of people I was dealing with. In my naïveté I had identified them with what I saw of them. Hitler could rant and rave when he was involved in politics, but that was part of his job; aside from that he was courtesy incarnate, just like a professional boxer who doesn't floor anyone out of the ring. I was once given a jovial wink by Göring, and I remember that that dreadful Heydrich once pulled a rose out of a vase at lunch and handed it gallantly to Julia. Do you remember, Julia?"

She nodded without looking at them.

"I had shut myself off from everything else they did. Of course I suspected that terrible things were happening, because you sometimes picked things up, but I didn't want to know. I did not even talk about it to Julia. Only Bormann, who could never relax, always had a sinister air about him, though he was not the biggest criminal in the bunch."

"But he was enough of a criminal to blackmail you with the death of your wife, wasn't he?"

"Of course. He was an extension of Hitler."

"Like the others."

"That's true. Hitler had turned almost the whole German people into himself, and he intended to do the same with the whole of mankind. His followers did exactly what he wanted, even without orders. They were able to destroy people because they had first been destroyed as human beings themselves by him."

"You put that very well, Mr. Falk. And where did things go from there?"

"It must look like an accident. There would be no inquest, because why should I murder my own son? I must think up something for myself. It must not be within the next week—of course so that no one would make a connection with Bormann's presence—and no later than in two weeks' time. Then he said 'Heil Hitler,' and I was dismissed."

Herter pulled a face. "Do you realize that what you are saying is making me feel sick? What on earth got into those people? Did you discuss it with your wife?"

Julia had taken another drag on her cigarette, and at every word some pale blue smoke escaped from her mouth, as if from a creature of fable. "He only told me what had happened at the end of the war, after we had heard on the radio in The Hague that Hitler was dead."

"One day after he had married Eva Braun," said Herter. "How in heaven's name is it all possible? For some reason he wanted Siegfried murdered—who knows?—because he had discovered that he was not the father?—and finally he marries the mother, who may have deceived him but whom he has allowed to live. I can't make head or tail of it. Obviously something completely different happened."

Falk raised both hands for a moment and dropped them limply onto his thighs. "Mysteries, mysteries. You won't find an explanation by thinking about it. No one will ever get to the bottom of it. There is no one left alive who could say."

"And you, too? Were you not in danger as well? Didn't you know too much?"

"I wasn't frightened of that," said Falk. "Otherwise they wouldn't have dreamed up such a complicated plan. In that case they would simply have murdered all three of us; the gentlemen had no problem with that, certainly in such a hermetically sealed place as the Berghof. No, obviously they trusted us, and we had found mercy in their eyes because we had looked after Siggi so well."

"How in heaven's name did you get through those days?"

Falk sighed and shook his head. "When I think back, I see nothing at all. After the war I once had a car accident and was concussed, and I couldn't remember anything about that."

Small and old, Julia and he sat on the worn-out sofa, under Brueghel's four-hundred-year-old gluttonous feast, like two hyperrealistic statues by an American artist.

"Of course I wanted nothing better than to talk to Julia about it," he continued, "but what was the point? Why should I burden her with something so horrific, which nothing could be done about anyway? I had to choose between one or three dead people—the only way of escaping was flight, preferably all three of us. But that was completely impossible: no one could enter the Führer's zone on the Obersalzberg, but neither could they leave it. There were sentry posts everywhere. Anyway, Bormann had naturally given instructions for reinforcement of the guard. I considered involving Dr. Krüger, because he was a decent man; perhaps he could smuggle us out in his DKW, but then I would have had to phone him, and of course the telephone was tapped. Apart from which, I would have endangered his life by doing that. No, the situation was hopeless. Whichever way I looked at it, I had no choice. I had to do it, for Julia. So it must appear to be an accident for her, too."

There was another silence. Herter tried to imagine murdering his little Marnix because otherwise not only he but Maria, too, would have to die. The very thought made him feel ill. What would he do? Probably he would have reached the conclusion with Maria that all three of them might as well die. How could one go on living after such an act, even if carried out under compulsion? But perhaps the difference lay in the fact that Marnix was their own child.

"Do you want to hear?" asked Falk.

No, he didn't want to hear, but Falk wanted to tell the story. Herter made a scarcely visible motion of his head, whereupon Julia got up and went to the bedroom. When she had shut the door behind her, Falk closed his eyes and did not open them again during the whole of his account. As if Herter were also enveloped in the darkness behind those eyelids, in which Falk again saw the drama unfolding, he listened to the faint voice, feeling as if the Eben Haëzer Home were sinking into oblivion and through the words he was physically present at the events of the story, there in that doomed spot, destroyed over half a century ago—seeing everything, hearing everything. . . .

A minute before his alarm clock goes off, Falk opens his eyes. He immediately starts sweating. Today. He has imagined it countless times during those two weeks, but now that the moment has come, it is completely different. He turns the alarm off and looks at the back of Julia's head. She is asleep, breathing peacefully. Confused and shivering all over, he gets out of bed and opens the curtains. A chilly, gray autumn morning, the summits of the Alps now invisible in the approaching winter. The world has changed its aspect. He feels like someone who is mortally ill and has decided that today is to be his last day. Soon the doctor will come in secret with his syringe. He is still asleep now, the friendly doctor who is prepared to take a risk, or he is reading the morning paper with a cup of coffee in his hand. Russian offensive in the Memel region. For as long as he can remember, people have been dying in huge numbers. Dying has become insignificant. *The Führer's orders have the force of law.* The irrevocability of that law is harder than the granite of the Alps. In a few hours he will have to obey it.

With a yawn Julia turns onto her back and folds her hands behind her head.

"Is something wrong, Ullrich?"

"I didn't sleep well."

"Is Siggi already awake?"

"I think I heard something. I promised I'd show him the firing range today. He's been pestering me for weeks about it."

With a sigh Julia throws off the blankets and gets out of bed.

"Why are you men always so crazy about that stupid violence? If Siggi had been a girl, she wouldn't have pestered you about it."

"That difference has a long history, I think."

Siggi is already dressed. In his chamois leather Tyrolean shorts with the horn buttons, he is sitting on the floor, slowly moving a red magnet around his compass.

"Look, Daddy, that needle has gone crazy. Do you know why that is? Because the magnet is horseshoe-shaped. The needle wants to tear itself free and be happy, because a horseshoe brings luck, but it is tied, just like a dog on a chain."

Marnix. That is exactly how Marnix might have put it.

That child! Falk feels as if his veins are filled with molten lead. He himself has never had such an idea in the thirty-three years he has been alive. What kind of world is this? Surely it's not conceivable that in a short while he will destroy that little life! Should he not grab his pistol right away and shoot himself in the head? And what about Julia, then? Suddenly he remembers the one and only time that he had previously shot at anyone, nine years ago in the Vienna Chancellery, during the failed coup. In the chaos and din of gunfire, shouting, exploding hand grenades, and shattering glass, he suddenly saw Dollfuss lying on his face on the carpet, groaning and calling for a priest: he recognized him immediately, for the chancellor was only slightly bigger than Siggi. He was bleeding from a large wound below his left ear. At that moment the violence took hold of Ullrich, too, and before he knew it, he had also fired a shot. A few days later, Otto Planetta confessed to the first, probably fatal shot; within a week he was sentenced and hanged. The second shot, with a different caliber, has always remained a mystery and is still speculated about. From shame he had never told anyone about it, not even Julia, not even when those involved in the coup were honored as heroes after the annexation, not even after the war. He tried to pretend to himself that it had been a coup de grâce; when that failed, he buried it in himself and never thought about it again.

He puts on his pistol and goes to the kitchen, where Siggi is stirring a knob of butter and half a bar of milk chocolate into his porridge, as he has learned from his father. The condemned prisoner's last meal. Why bother to eat? He won't even have time to digest it. Time! Julia has lit up her first Ukraina cigarette and sings softly as she moves about:

> *"Everything will pass by now,*
> *Everything will pass. . . ."*

Time is harder than the granite that surrounds the house; not even a scratch can be made in it. The realization that she is seeing the child for the last time, without knowing, cuts him even more to the quick than the thought of what he must do in a few moments.

"We must go."

"Put your scarf on, too, Siggi, don't catch cold. And for goodness' sake be careful, you two."

When they go outside, the air is full of glittering icicles, which seem to be hanging still in the chilly air.

"Look, Daddy, the Mother of Our Lord has dropped her pincushion."

A sob goes through Falk's chest, and he takes Siggi's hand. As they climb up the alpine meadow, the boy constantly makes wild leaps, as if he wants to fly. Among the firs they are halted with a "Heil Hitler" by a patrolling SS man with a German shepherd on a lead and a rifle over his shoulder.

After Falk has shown his pass, issued to him by Mittl-strasser, Siggi asks, "Daddy, how was water made?"

"I don't know."

"Do you think Uncle Wolf knows?"

"I'm sure he does. Uncle Wolf always knows everything."

"But he doesn't know that Auntie Effi smokes when he's not there."

"Perhaps even that."

The sound of bellowed orders becomes audible, but it does not seem to get through to Siggi. As they walk on, he looks thoughtfully at the ground and a little later says, "But if you know everything, how do you know that it's really 'everything'?"

"I don't know that either, Siggi."

"I know a lot, too, but how can I find out all that I know?"

Falk does not answer. This torture! The world should not exist, the world is a terrible mistake, an absurd miscarriage—so absurd that nothing, absolutely nothing matters. Everything will be forgotten and finally disappear and will never have happened. And it is this thought that suddenly gives him the perverted strength to do what he has to do. He takes a deep breath and lets go of Siggi's hand.

The large parade ground is surrounded by barracks, canteens, garages, and administration buildings. Flanked by a swastika flag and a black SS flag, helmeted troops are on parade and move with the same discipline as the Chief's body, when he is in public. Via the gym they go down a flight of steps to the underground firing ranges, and Falk thinks, what difference does it make that he has seen daylight for the last time? A steel door, whose main function is to ensure that the Chief is not disturbed in his world-historical reflections, closes behind them.

"Perhaps this is not really the place for children," says the duty Obersturmführer, shaking his head in the booming and rattling, after reading Mittlstrasser's document. "Well, everything's one big mess in Germany these days."

Yes, of course Mittlstrasser is in the plot, or maybe not; it's all the same to Falk. Siggi is excited by the pandemonium in the concrete area and shouts something that Falk cannot understand. On the longest of the three firing ranges, about a hundred yards long, two soldiers in battle dress, bathed in harsh electric light, are lying behind juddering machine guns, while instructors with binoculars monitor their results. The second range, in which rifles are used, is shorter; the third, shorter still, is not in use.

A passing Unterscharführer yells, in passing, with a glance at Siggi, "Has that age group been called up already?"

Falk produces his loaded 7.65 pistol and shows Siggi the magazine containing the bullets. He stands with his feet apart, holds the weapon with both hands, and fires a shot, which hits the schematic figure at the end of the range in the belly, at which Siggi cries, "Can I have a go, too? Can I have a go, too?"

The world does not exist. None of it is true. Nothing exists. He drops to one knee and demonstrates how the pistol must be held. As a joke he points the barrel from close range at Siggi's forehead. When Siggi begins to laugh, he pulls the trigger.

Spattered with blood, he remains staring at the point where Siggi's laugh was a moment ago. No one has seen or heard anything. He closes his eyes and slowly lowers the weapon, until the barrel touches the motionless body, thinking—It wasn't me who killed him. Hitler killed him. Not me, Hitler. I. Hitler.

FIFTEEN

Herter leaned forward, his elbows on his knees, his hands over his eyes. When the talking stopped, he looked up as if waking from a dream. It seemed as if it were now the room that had changed into something unreal. In the courtyard a dog barked. Falk had also opened his eyes; his hands were trembling. Herter could see that the old man was exhausted, but also somehow liberated. As a result of his gruesome story, everything had simply become even more incomprehensible, but at the same time it was proof that it was true, since otherwise the storyteller would have made everything fit neatly in place. Involuntarily he glanced at Falk's right index finger, with which he had pulled the trigger fifty-five years ago and had to force himself not to look at the photograph on the television set. Siegfried Falk would have been sixty-one now, without knowing who he was; on certain days, with his wife and children, he would have visited his parents in Eben Haëzer.

Falk got up, opened the door of the bedroom door a fraction, and sat down again. Perhaps he had spoken so softly to spare Julia what she already knew.

A little later she appeared and asked, "Would you like a glass of wine perhaps?"

Yes, wine, he was ready for some of that now. Most of all he would have liked to get drunk and free himself of that haunted castle, as Falk had called it, compared with which Count Dracula's was an idyllic country seat—but at the same time he knew that he would not be able to, any more than the Falks. Now the Obersalzberg site was impossible to find and completely overgrown with trees and bushes, through which certain kinds of tourists tried to find a way—but only in reality, not where it really mattered.

In silence they sipped the cheap supermarket wine, which was too sweet and no more than one glass of which must be drunk. Herter felt that he should say something first, but what more was there to say? He shook his head.

"I have never heard a more shocking or more unsatisfactory story. I can only repeat what I said, Mr. Falk. I am speechless."

"You don't have to say anything. I'm grateful to you for being willing to listen to me. You have helped us a great deal."

"Yes," said Julia, looking into her glass.

So now he could get up and take his leave, but that would be too abrupt.

"What happened afterward?"

"The following day we received a telegram of condolence from Bormann, on behalf of the Führer."

Herter sighed and was silent for a moment. "Where was Siggi buried?"

"In the cemetery of Berchtesgaden, three days later. There

were just a few of us: Julia's parents, Mittlstrasser, Mrs. Köppe, and a few other members of the staff. The comedy continued, with us as grieving parents."

Julia looked up. "But that's what we were, in fact."

"Of course that's what we were, Julia. That's what we still are."

Herter glanced from one to the other. There seemed to be a point of friction here.

"Did you visit his grave later?" he asked Julia.

"No. There was going to be a headstone with his name on it, but by that time we had already been transferred."

"To The Hague, that is."

"Yes, just a week later. Mittlstrasser said that different surroundings would help us to forget the tragic accident."

"Did Seyss-Inquart know the full story?"

"I don't know," said Falk. "I don't think so. The first thing he did when he met us was to express his condolences at our loss. What reason could they have had to let him in on the secret?"

"None." Herter nodded. "For Hitler, Seyss-Inquart was just a lowly subordinate, even though he had delivered Austria to him."

The mobile telephone in his breast pocket vibrated. "Yes?"

"It's me. Where have you got to?"

"To the war."

"You won't forget our plane?"

"I'll be right back." He ended the call and could finally look at his watch again: three-thirty. "That was my girlfriend. She's worried we'll miss our plane."

"You're going back to Amsterdam today?"

"Yes."

"I was there once," said Falk, getting up, "in the middle of the so-called Hunger Winter. Everything was still standing, but it was a burned-out, fatally wounded city. I remember that the canals were full of floating rubbish from one side to the other."

Before getting up himself, Herter took the copy of *The Invention of Love* and with his fountain pen wrote on the title page:

For Ullrich Falk,
who in the days of evil
made an unimaginable sacrifice
to love.
And for Julia.
Rudolf Herter
Vienna, November 1999

He blew on it for a moment and closed the book, so that they would not read it until he had gone.

"Do you have a visiting card?" asked Falk.

"I haven't made it that far yet," said Herter, "but I'll write it down for you." On a page from his notebook, he noted down his address and telephone number and tore the page out. "You can always write to me or phone me—at my expense, of course."

"I shall give this to Mrs. Brandstätter and tell her to let you know when the last of the two of us has died. After that you are free to do or not do whatever you want."

Herter shook his head. "You won't be dying for a long time yet, I can see that. You've almost started the next century."

"This one's enough for us," said Julia stiffly.

They said good-bye. Herter kissed Julia's hand and thanked Falk for confiding in him.

"On the contrary," said Falk, "we thank *you*. If you had not been prepared to listen to us, nothing at all would have been left of Siggi. It would have been as if he had never existed."

SIXTEEN

When he arrived back in the hotel room, Maria was packing. He closed the door behind him and said, "I've understood him."

"Who?" she asked, straightening up from bending over the case on the bed.

"Him!"

"You look a bit disheveled, Rudi. What's happened?"

"Too much. I'm beaten. The imagination counts for nothing. Exit Otto."

"Otto? Who is Otto?"

"Don't bother, he no longer exists. There will be no *Enemy of Light*. The imagination cannot challenge reality; reality bats the imagination into the stratosphere and roars with laughter."

"Have you been drinking, by any chance?"

"A glass of cheap wine, but now I want a glass of nectar to drink to Minerva's owl, which flies out at dusk."

"What on earth are you going on about?" asked Maria, kneeling down at the minibar.

"That insight is a melancholy dessert to creativity, a poor consolation for those who fail."

"Fortunately I know you. Otherwise I would think you were just ranting. I don't think you look well."

"I am mortally sad."

"Lie down for a bit."

He shoved the case aside and did as she had said.

"Did you learn anything from those old people?"

"Those old people, as you call them, were the personal servants of Hitler and Eva Braun, and I learned something earth-shattering, something completely unbelievable and blood-curdling and at the same time utterly incredible—but I swore with two fingers raised that I would not tell anyone while they are still alive."

"Not even me?"

"The problem is that you're someone, too."

"But what if you're run over by a streetcar tomorrow?"

"Then no one will ever know. But I shall write it all down at home and deposit it with the lawyer. Get me the dictating machine—it's over there next to my eyedrops. There's someone who is no one, and I've just got to get my thoughts in order about that person."

"It would be better if you had a quarter of an hour's sleep."

"No. If I do, it may slip through my fingers."

Maria switched the machine on and gave it to him.

He thought for a moment, brought it to his mouth, and said at dictation speed, "Hitler's chief of staff, General Jodl, who spent hours with him every day, once said that for him the Führer always remained a closed book. Today I have opened the book. It turns out to be a dummy, with nothing but empty pages. He was a walking abyss. The last word on Hitler is 'nothing.' All those countless essays on his person fall short, because they are about something, not about nothing. It was not that he did not let anyone get close, as everyone says who knew him, but that there was nothing to get close to. Or no, perhaps I should put it the other way around. Perhaps the way to see it was that the vacuum that he was sucked into was itself full of other people, who as a result were also destroyed. In that direction, then, lies the explanation for the inhuman acts of his morally dehumanized followers. In fact, the whole thing now reminds me of a black hole—a monstrous astronomical object, a pathological deformation of space and time, created by the catastrophic collapse of a heavy star, a maw that devours everything that comes near it—matter, radiation, everything—from which nothing can escape. Even light is caught in its gravitational field, all information is cut off from the rest of the world—it is true that it *glows*, but nothing can be concluded from that amorphous heat. In its center is a so-called singularity. This is a paradoxical entity of infinite density and infinitely high temperature, with a volume of zero. Hitler as a singularity in human form—surrounded by the black hole of his retinue! If you ask me, no one has yet come up with that idea. Right. I am not going to give this all-devouring Nothingness a psychological foundation, as is always attempted in vain, but a philosophical one, since it is first and foremost a *logical* problem: a cluster of predicates without a subject. This makes it the exact opposite of the God in the negative theology of Pseudo-Dionysius Areopagita, from the fifth century: in that God is a subject without predicates, since he is too big for us to be able to say anything about him. So you could assert that, in the framework of negative theology, Hitler is the devil—but not in the official, positive theology of Augustine and Aquinas. Anyway, enough."

He drank a mouthful of the Chablis that Maria had put beside him and continued into the machine:

"Pay attention, the excursion becomes even more instructive. In the wake of Hegel, but in opposition to him, Kierkegaard said that Nothingness gives birth to fear. He wrote of Nero that he was a mystery to himself and that his essence was fear: that was why he wanted to be a mystery to everyone and revel in their fear. Later Heidegger turned Kierkegaard's proposition on its head and said that fear reveals Nothingness—and that 'in the Being of being the annihilation of Nothingness' takes place. Jeering laughter from the logical positivists, of course, especially the Vienna Circle, with Carnap at their head—but does not the explanation of Hitler lie in the direction of that negativistic conception? That is, as the personification of that angst-creating, annihilating Nothingness, the exterminator of everything and everyone, not only of his enemies but also of his friends, not only of the Jews, the Gypsies, the Poles, the Russians, the mentally defective, and so on and so on but also of the Germans, his wife, his dog, and finally himself? Perhaps in this case Carnap should first have thought of his favorite science: mathematics. In it the paradoxical number zero is nothing less than a natural number, which through multiplication destroys every other number. In mathematics the function of zero is to zero—the zero is the Hitler among numbers. Is it at the same time a possible explanation for Heidegger's metaphysical fraternization with that zero among human beings, whom he, suffering from a case of optical illusion, had taken to be the personification of Being? After all, the philosopher with the nightcap and admirer of the 'primeval rock, granite, hard will' such as you see on the Obersalzberg, had an SA uniform hanging in his wardrobe. And then there is Sartre, who is part of the same tradition, but with whom things land on their feet again when he wrote that the anti-Semite is a person who wants to be a stubborn, hard rock, a seething river, a devastating flash of lightning—everything except a human being. And in the background of all this is the vague ecstatic form of Meister Eckehart, whose mystical obsession, seen from this perspective, suddenly takes on demonic features, he, with his 'dark night of the soul' and becoming nothing . . . which is subsequently monstrously staged in the black hole of the party rallies in Nuremberg, after sunset, surrounded by pillars of light that merge with the starry sky, with Hitler as the paradoxical singularity in the center of thousands of men in uniform, the only one bareheaded. . . ." Herter shivered. "I'm shivering, but that shivering of course points precisely in the right direction: that of the horrific, the ghastly, the *mysterium tremendum ac fascinans*."

"The what?" asked Maria with her head cocked to one side.

"Hey, are you eavesdropping on me, by any chance?"

"I can't help it, but don't worry. Probably new worlds open up to you when you say these kinds of things, but I understand less than half. Should I go?"

"No, of course not. On the contrary, it's good if someone listens with me."

"I thought it was secret."

"I'm not going to be talking about that secret, only about the explanation of the secret that Hitler was."

The *mysterium tremendum ac fascinans*, he explained, was a term that had been coined over eighty years ago by Rudolf

Otto, in his book *The Idea of the Holy*. Herter had reread it a few weeks ago, obviously because of a kind of premonition. As a young man, Nietzsche had written *The Birth of Tragedy from the Spirit of Music*, which Herter had been talking about only yesterday. In that book he supplemented the "noble simplicity and silent grandeur" of Winckelmann's Apollonian, peaceful, harmonious vision of Greek culture with its Dionysian, ecstatic, irrational, terrifying counterpart. You could say that following on from that, Rudolf Otto had pointed to the core of all religion: the terrifying "Totally Other," the absolutely foreign, the denial of everything that exists and can be thought, the mystical Nothingness, the stupor, the sense of being "knocked out cold" that both attracts and repels. That was a different tune from the Christians' benign "dear Lord." He was an asthmatic descendant of the authentic, wild heavenly men and women—who, by the way, did not shrink from sacrificing his own son, an act he had once forbidden Abraham from committing. No, only Hitler was the epiphany of that chilling tradition.

"I'm doing my best," said Maria.

In the course of time, he continued, countless experts had racked their brains over the question of when Adolf became Hitler. First he was an innocent infant, then a delightful toddler, then a growing child, then a young man eager to learn—where, when, how, as a result of what had he changed into absolute terror? No one had yet given a satisfactory answer. Why not? Perhaps because the psychologists were not philosophers, and especially not theologians. And perhaps in turn the monotheistic theologians gave Hitler a wide berth and became caught up in theodicy: how could the one God allow Auschwitz? Yes, he was suddenly sure of it. None of the theologians dared go to the ultimate extreme, like Hitler himself. Fear of the Totally Other had paralyzed them, too. Hitler had knocked them out cold, too—some even regarded it as immoral to try to understand him. But now Hitler found him, Herter, on his path.

"Perhaps, Rudi," said Maria, interrupting him thoughtfully, "it would be sensible to stop. Aren't you frightened of being knocked out cold yourself?"

He shook his head. "I can't go back anymore; it's too late. I have realized why Hitler is incomprehensible and will always remain so: because he was incomprehensibility in person—that is, in nonperson. An old star changes through particular causes into a singularity surrounded by a black hole, but Hitler did not change at a certain moment in his life into that infernal horror—for example, through the violence of his revolting father or the grisly death from cancer of his mother, who was treated by a Jewish doctor, or a gas attack in the First World War, which left him temporarily blind. Other people have been through worse horrors and yet not become Hitlers. They simply did not fulfill the preconditions that Hitler did before he had experienced anything at all—precisely the absence of all values. It was not a specific experience that ate away his soul; he was terror itself from his very birth. Nero had the status of a god, but that was an apotheosis conferred one day on Nero the human being by other human beings: all positive facts. But Hitler was from the very beginning the manifestation of the Totally Other: the zeroing Zero incarnate, the living singularity, who of necessity would become visible only as a mask. This made him therefore no actor, not a thespian, as he is commonly regarded, but a mask with no face behind it: a living mask. A walking suit of armor, with no one inside." He thought for a moment of Julia, who, unlike her husband, had seen only an actor in him.

"So according to you, he was unique," said Maria with her eyebrows raised skeptically.

Herter sighed. "Yes, I've a nasty feeling that he was unique."

"He thought that himself. So he was right."

"Yes, we must finally face up to the fact. Except that there was no question of a 'self.' That's why you can't really call him 'guilty'; that is already according him too much honor and shows a lack of appreciation of his zero-value status. But I understand what you mean. With such a paradoxically inhuman nature as his, something unbearably sacred clings to him, albeit in a negative sense. That is acceptable only if it can be proved in some way. But how can 'nothing' be proved? How can something supernatural be 'proved'?"

Suddenly he sat up straight, stared ahead with his eyes wide. To his dismay—but at the same time to his joy, for such is the dubious nature of thought—something occurred to him that seemed to come close to a proof.

"Wait a moment. . . . Damn it, Maria, I believe I'm making a discovery," he said into the cassette recorder, as if it were called Maria. "It's too crazy for words, but perhaps . . . I'm excited, I must take it easy, easy, easy, step for step, the ice is slippery. . . . Listen. A thousand years ago Anselm of Canterbury came up with a crushing proof of God's existence, which is more or less: God is perfect; therefore he exists; otherwise he would not exist. Later Kant called that the 'ontological proof,' but of course it is no such thing, since it appears only to make the transition from thought to real existence. *On* means 'what exists' in Greek. It is more a 'logical proof of God.' But now I really think that I have hold of its mirror image: a truly onto-logical proof for the proposition that Hitler was the manifesta-tion of the nonexistent, annihilating Nothingness."

Maria looked at him ironically. "That's a whole mouthful for precious little."

"Well, how am I supposed to say the unsayable?"

"Didn't Wittgenstein say that you should be silent about it?"

"That means you never make any progress. Another Vien-nese, by the way. I am not going to be silenced by Viennese; my father was the last person with the power to do that, but not for very long."

"It's as if you still can't stand it."

Herter shook his head impatiently. "For God's sake, leave psychology out of it, Maria. Nothing ever gets better. Right, here we go. I need to take a run at it."

The drama of the twentieth century, he lectured, began with Plato and his installation of a World of Ideas beyond the visible one. That led directly to Kant's unknowable thing in itself. After him the development split into two currents, an optimistic one and a pessimistic one. The optimistic one was Hegel's rationalist, dialectic method, which led via Marx to Stalin—or, perhaps it would be fair to say, to Gorbachev. As he already asserted, the tradition of Nothingness also started from Hegel, with Kierkegaard, Heidegger, and Sartre as an existen-tialist side branch; he must think a little more about how it pre-cisely fitted together. The founding father of the pessimistic, irrational current was Schopenhauer. With him the eternal thing in itself evolved into a dogmatic, dynamic "Will," which ruled the whole world, including the orbits of the planets, and which in the individual had taken the form of his body.

He looked at Maria. "Can you feel that we're getting close?"

"To tell you the truth . . ."

"No, let me go on, before I lose the thread. When you've typed it out, I'll explain it. And pour me another glass, because we're approaching the heart of the matter: music."

Since Plato, Herter said, who, in the spirit of Pythagoras, had the world created according to the laws of musical harmony, no one had played greater homage to music than Schopenhauer. For him it was nothing less than the illustration of his world Will. If anyone were to succeed, he once wrote, to express in concepts what music was, that would be at the same time the explanation of the world—that is, the true philosophy. Two more steps, said Herter, and he would be where he wanted to be. First step: Richard Wagner. The great composer of enchanting operas was both a lifelong follower of Schopenhauer and also an anti-Semite of a new kind. The Jews must not merely be combated and restricted because they supposedly had disproportionate power and influence in all fields of civilization, as traditional anti-Semites had been saying since time immemorial and still are, resulting in an incidental pogrom here and there—no, he was the first to proclaim in his writing that they had no right to exist, that they should disappear without exception off the face of the earth. With him the metaphysical anti-Semitism of extermination was born. Not even by having themselves baptized could they rid themselves of the curse upon them, as the Christians and Muslims conceded. He tried in vain to harness his devoted admirer, the unstable King Ludwig II of Bavaria, to his bloodthirsty bandwagon, but Ludwig found Wagner's rabid anti-Semitism vulgar—proving that he wasn't so unstable after all.

The recorder switched itself off with a click.

SEVENTEEN

"Our plane leaves at eight-thirty," said Maria, turning the tiny tape for him.

"Bags of time."

"You've still got to pack."

"It will all be fine," he said impatiently. "If necessary, we'll miss the flight."

"You do know that Olga and Marnix are meeting us? He thought it was wonderful being able to stay up so late."

"We can always phone them and put it off." He switched the machine on again, put a finger briefly to his lips, and said, "Right. Second step. Nietzsche. Now things get difficult. He, too, was a follower of Schopenhauer as a young man, and in addition an admiring houseguest of Wagner's. He wrote enthusiastic pieces about both, but as his own ideas developed, he distanced himself from them. Schopenhauer's abstract Will underlay the Dionysian primeval force in *The Birth of Tragedy from the Spirit of Music*, which as a twenty-seven-year-old he had dedicated to Wagner in 1871. I know all that very exactly; I read him when I was no more than nineteen, just after the war; I think I identified with him a little at the time. At the end of the short period in which Nietzsche had his sanity, seventeen years later, Schopenhauer's musical Will became even more concrete in his own Will to Power. Add the two quotations here," he said, suddenly toneless, in a deeper voice.

"What's that?" asked Maria, again cocking her head slightly again.

"Don't worry. It's something I want to insert later."

He had once made an astonishing discovery. In the passage where Schopenhauer talks of the hypothetical translation of music into true philosophy, he says literally ". . . *that supposing that it were possible to give a totally accurate and complete explanation of music that dealt with particulars, that is, an extensive repetition of what it expresses in concepts, that would immediately be a sufficient repetition and explanation of the world in concepts, or one that is identical, and hence the true philosophy. . . .*" Decades later the complicated melody of that sentence returns in Nietzsche: "*Supposing finally that it were possible to explain the whole of our instinctual life as the representation and suppression of a basic form of Will—namely the Will to Power, as is my proposition; supposing that one could trace back all organic functions to this Will to Power and could also find in it the solution to the problem of procreation and nourishment—it is a problem—would have thereby have earned the right to determine all active force unambiguously as: Will to Power.*" As far as Herter knew, the chromatic similarity of those two crucial texts had never struck anyone before. Had it struck Nietzsche himself? Was it a covert homage to Schopenhauer? Probably it was more an unconscious reminiscence of his reading of Schopenhauer. The "unconscious" . . . the last shoot, in Freud, from this murky family tree.

"Haven't you had enough of my lecture by now?" asked Herter.

"As if that would make any difference to you."

"That's true. By the time his Will to Power had dawned on him," he continued, "Nietzsche had already put a few other shocking things on the agenda in his *Thus Spake Zarathustra*, such as the concept of the Superman, the domination of the strong over the weak, the abolition of pity, and the assertion that God is dead. Yes, he had quite some nerve. The deeply unhappy Fritz *suffered* under his own daring; what he most wanted was that someone should demonstrate that his ideas were wrong."

Maria looked at him sharply and asked, "Am I seeing things, or are there tears in your eyes?"

Herter put the cassette recorder aside for a minute and rubbed his eyes. "Yes, you're right."

"Why, for heaven's sake? I always understood that his brain waves inspired Hitler."

"In that case you understood incorrectly, and you're not the only one. He was the first *victim* of Hitler."

"If you ask me, Hitler wasn't even born at that time."

"You're right. And there you immediately touch on the point that I am after. Listen," he said, picking up the recorder again, "I'll try to explain, to myself, too. I can't quite believe it myself yet. Nietzsche died at the end of August 1900: exactly a century ago next year. By that time he was completely mad, finally more of a vegetable than a human being, nursed first by his mother, then by his sister. How did that outbreak of madness proceed? Pay attention. I'm going to look more carefully at the dates. I haven't got everything to hand, but I do have them in broad outline—I'll chase everything up at home: I'm already looking forward to that. What can be finer than to have to study in the wake of an idea? I've never been able to study without an idea, not even at school. Right. When he wrote his *Zarathustra*, in the first half of the 1880s, he was still perfectly mentally in order. In the next few years, he published a number of important titles. In addition he wrote down in this period more than a thousand aphorisms, which were intended to lead to a philosophical counterpart of *Zarathustra* but that never materialized. In the summer of the year 1888, when the preparatory work had probably been done, things went wrong, like a cloud passing across the sun. After his death the material was arranged by his rather fraudulent sister and published under the title *The Will to Power*, and in that form it had a huge influence. It is more a prophet than a philosopher talking: he calls himself a 'prophetic bird spirit.' He said that he was writing the history of the next two centuries; we are now halfway, and in the first quarter everything was exactly as he predicted. It happened faster than he thought. Or perhaps we should say that the twenty-first century will also be under the spell of Hitler. The corrupt edition of Elisabeth Förster-Nietzsche begins with the famous sentence 'Nihilism is at the door; where does this most horrific of all guests come from?' Isn't that odd? Here nihilism appears as a guest, as a person. That has always been regarded as a stylistic flourish, but I read it differently now. The term 'nihilism' is derived from *nihil*, 'nothing'—so what is being said, in a nutshell, is, 'Hitler is at the door.'"

"Do you know what I think, Rudi?" said Maria. "That you're making yourself ill."

"I suspect Nietzsche was sometimes told that, too."

"And because he didn't listen, he came to a bad end."

"Exactly. And I'm going to explain to you how that may be Hitler's doing. It's the summer of 1888. Suddenly a shadow obscures the sun, and he puts aside his notes for *The Will to Power* and in the following months publishes in rapid succession a number of studies in which the destruction of his mind is clearer and clearer. Wagner, the arch-anti-Semite, is once again given both barrels; he writes sentences like 'I shall simply have all anti-Semites shot,' and in his autobiographical sketch *Ecce Homo*, he says that all the great figures of world literature could not have written one speech of *Zarathustra* between them. He regards himself as the successor of the dead God and wants to introduce a new calendar. Everything becomes increasingly megalomaniac: he signs letters 'Dionysus,' 'the Crucified One,' 'Antichrist,' and in his final, posthumously published notes of January 1889, he shows himself ready to rule the world. Then night finally falls on his mind. When he passes a cab stand in Turin, like the one opposite here, he sees a coachman mistreating his old horse with a whip. He rushes up, and he, the great despiser of pity, falls around the horse's neck in floods of tears. . . ."

For a moment Herter could not continue and felt his eyes again filling with tears. Maria got up, glanced at the carriages on the square, and sat down next to him on the bed.

He cleared his throat and said, "The director of the psychiatric clinic to which he was admitted was called Dr. Wille."

"What a coincidence."

"What a coincidence indeed. And there are more coincidences. In his view and that of all later doctors, the patient was suffering from a progressive, postsyphilitic paralysis."

"But?" asked Maria.

He looked at her. His hand holding the recorder was trembling slightly. "Do you know when Hitler was born?"

"Of course not."

"On April 20, 1889." He sat up. "Do you realize what that means?" And when she raised her eyes in a questioning expression: "That he was conceived in July 1888—exactly at the moment when Nietzsche's decline began. And when he was born nine months later, Friedrich Nietzsche had ceased to exist. The brain in which all those thoughts had arisen was destroyed in the months when their personification, no, *de*personification was growing in the womb. That is my ontological proof of Nothingness."

Maria's mouth dropped open slightly. "Rudi, you're not crazy enough to—"

"Yes I am crazy enough. His destruction was not *paralysis progressiva* but Adolf Hitler."

Speechless, Maria stared at him. "I'm starting to doubt your state of mind, too. It's all complete coincidence!"

"Oh? And when does coincidence stop being coincidence? If someone throws a six a hundred times in succession with the dice, is that still coincidence? In the strict sense yes, since no one throw has anything to do with the preceding one; still, it has never yet happened. You can happily bet your bottom dollar that if it did happen, the dice were loaded. Check it out. On the one hand we have Nietzsche, who writes prophetically on all the things I mentioned, and on the other Hitler, who fulfills them. A few days before his final collapse—when Hitler was six months old—Nietzsche wrote literally that he knew his fate: that his name would one day be linked to something monstrous, to a crisis such as there had never been on earth, to the deepest conflict of conscience, to a decision, taken *against* everything that had been believed, demanded, held sacred up to then. At the time no one could understand what he was talking about, but now we know. It was Hitler who took the predicted 'monstrous decision': it turned out to be his central obsession—the *Final Solution of the Jewish Question*—their physical extermination, which Wagner had been the first to threaten them with and precisely what Nietzsche despised in him. From a childhood friend we know, by the way, that the future murderer of peoples hung on every word of Wagner's anti-Semitic writings. Hitler also read Nietzsche as a young man, but, significantly, the unstoppable young talker did not want to discuss him with his friend; of course, because it was too close to the bone. Anyway, he was not that fond of philosophy and literature; his passions were architecture and the musical theater, especially Wagner, and even there mainly the sets and staging. In a different way only Nietzsche was as obsessed with Wagner as Hitler was. Apart from that Hitler, too, had decided to rule the world, he also toyed with the idea of a new calendar, and so on and so on—I could continue for a lot longer. With Hitler, Nietzsche's megalomania and his anxieties became reality from A to Z; it all fits like a glove. Later, when as chancellor he was visiting Nietzsche's sister in Leipzig, he even had something of a mystical experience there: it was as if, he said, he had seen her dead brother physically in the room and heard him speak. And is that precise coincidence of Hitler's origin and Nietzsche's downfall suddenly coincidental? And is it coincidental that they lived to be precisely the same age: fifty-six? Is it also coincidental that Nietzsche's madness lasted exactly as long as Hitler's time in power: twelve years?"

Maria raised her hands in a gesture of helplessness. "But how? How am I supposed to picture all this? What in heaven's name can a fetus in the belly of a woman in Austria have to do with the mental state of a man in Italy? It's too crazy for words!"

"It is, it is," said Herter, nodding his head quickly, "and yet it's true. Surely you can see with your own eyes. It's a grotesque miracle. He was never an innocent infant. Even as a fetus he was a murderer, and in a certain sense he always remained that murderous unborn child."

Maria almost screamed, "But *how then*, Rudi? For God's sake! How were those dice fixed? It's as if you've gone mad. What happened this afternoon at those old people's place? Come to your senses!"

"That's just what I'm doing, that's just what I'm doing. But not to reduce the matter to something everyday and then shrug my shoulders and turn away; but to go further, because this is not an everyday matter, for Christ's sake. Do you realize what we're talking about? We're talking about the worst thing imaginable. And the only thing I can think of is with Hitler we are dealing with something like a metanatural phenomenon—comparable with the impact of that meteorite in the Cretaceous period that wiped out the dinosaurs. Except that he was not an extraterrestrial creature but an extraexistential being: Nothingness."

Maria forced herself to be calm. "Okay, I'm trying to follow you. But I still don't understand it. Somewhere in an Austrian village . . . where was he born?"

"In Braunau."

"In Braunau, Hitler Senior crawls on top of his wife and comes, groaning with pleasure."

"Yes," said Herter. "Just imagine that. It all began with pleasure."

"And at that moment something starts to go wrong in Nietzsche's brain, hundreds of miles away in Turin."

"Yes. The night that fell in Nietzsche's mind was the darkness of the womb in which Hitler's body was taking shape."

"But that can't have been caused by that fertilized ovum in Braunau. At least I assume that you don't believe in some mysterious radiation."

"Of course not. There is a third way that caused both of them."

"Which is?"

Herter closed his eyes for a moment. "Nothing. That is precisely the miracle. After the death of God, Nothingness was at the door, and Hitler was its only born son. In a certain sense he never existed; he was, as it were, the *Hitler Lie* made flesh. The absolute, logical Antichrist."

"It's just as well no one but me can hear all the things you're saying. If you ask me, no one on earth can still follow you."

"That might be the proof that I'm on the right track. You must dare to think as ruthlessly about Hitler as he acts. I learned that from Nietzsche: he was before Hitler in the same way as I am after him." A strange, short laugh that mildly alarmed Maria escaped from his mouth. "Together we've caught him in a pincer movement. The circle is closed."

"And why did that Nothingness of yours precisely single out that family in Braunau?"

Herter turned his face away for a moment and sighed. "Why did Being choose that family in Nazareth at a particular moment at the beginning of our era? Hitler was more the founder of a religion than a politician. He said that he had been sent by providence, and the Germans *believed* in him—all his nocturnal mass rituals with torches and flags were religious in nature, all witnesses confirm that. The devil only knows; perhaps Klara Hitler was impregnated not by her Alois but by the Unholy Unspirit."

"Hitler has obviously converted you to the faith, too."

"Yes. Belief in Nothing, and Nietzsche is its prophet. And at the risk of your regarding me once and for all as mad, I'll tell you something else. Not only did he, with the destruction of his mind, represent Hitler's physical creation, not only did he herald in his writings much of Hitler's later philosophy; he also foresaw Hitler's end in detail. In one of his very last notes, entitled *Last Reflection*, he says literally, 'One may deliver the young criminal to me; I shall not hesitate to destroy him—I myself will make the torch flare up in his accursed spirit.' That referred to the German emperor. He died peacefully in Doorn in 1941, but four years later it befell his successor physically. In the bunker beneath the Chancellery, he shot himself in his right temple, Eva Braun took poison, after which their bodies were carried upstairs to the garden, hers by Bormann. There it was an inferno of bombing and shelling, the whistling of Soviet rocket launchers, the rattle of machine guns, smoke, stench, the screams of the wounded, the Russians, and all around, the city burned like Valhalla in *The Twilight of the Gods*. The bodies were laid in a grenade crater close to the exit and quickly had gasoline poured over them. Because no one dared venture into the ring of fire again, Adjutant Linge threw a burning cloth on top—and a policeman who saw the scene from a distance testified later that it was as if the flames flared up from their bodies of their own accord. Of their own accord! So that was Nietzsche's torch!"

Suddenly Herter's hand fell limply to his side, without switching off the recorder. "I can't keep my eyes open any longer."

"I can imagine," said Maria, who looked at her watch and got up. "Go and sleep for a bit; you've got half an hour or so. The embassy car will be here in an hour. I'll go downstairs and have a Viennese coffee—to bring me around. If you need me, just ring." She pressed a kiss on his closed eyes and left the room.

Herter felt as if he could sleep for a hundred years. Siegfried. He thought of the decorated *S*, the logo of the hotel that was repeated everywhere thousands of times: in the carpets in the corridors, on the coasters, the matchboxes, the bases of the lamps, the sachets of sugar, the pads by the telephones, the ballpoints, the cutlery, the ashtrays, the dressing gowns, the slippers . . . Siegfried . . . Siegfried . . . Siegfried . . .

To what extent was Hitler really a human being? He had the body of a man—although . . . there was something funny about that body from the start. At any rate in his description of "the Jew" who desired world domination in order to destroy mankind, he had given a strikingly realistic self-portrait. Herter thought of a sentence from *Mein Kampf* that had etched itself into his memory: *"If the Jew, with the aid of his Marxist creed, triumphs over the peoples of this world, his crown will be humanity's dance of death, and this planet, like it once did millions of years ago, will move through the ether empty of people."* Empty of people! In other words, the remaining Jews on the planet were not people—any more than he was. But his own dance of death was a degree more terrible still, since nowhere does he write that the victorious subhumans led by their verbal-mythical leader THE JEW would finally wipe themselves out, too, just as he did. And the fact that he chose precisely the Jews as the focus of his own nihilistic, total urge to destroy everything that existed was of course because of their realization of his own great ideal, the "racial purity" that they had managed to preserve for thousands of years.

He thought back to the Falks. What they had told him was undoubtedly true, but how could it be true? How could Eva, after Siggi's murder had been ordered, still become Mrs. Hitler and die with him? What was the necessity of that marriage? What was behind it, and what could have happened afterward? It was just as Falk had said: the answer could not be found by reflection.

Maria's question occurred to him again: why Nothingness had chosen Braunau of all places for Hitler's birthplace. That "brown" constantly recurred afterward: the party headquarters in Munich was called the "Brown House," the SA troopers were known as "brownshirts," and finally Eva's name was Braun, too. Because her family stayed so often on the Obersalzberg, Göring called the Berghof the "Braun house." Brown did not occur in the spectrum; it was a shit color that was created when you smeared all the colors of the spectrum together on a palette—and that thought reminded him of something that explained everything seamlessly. In Dr. Wille's clinic, the duty doctor noted of Nietzsche in the month of Hitler's birth, *"Often smears feces.—Wraps feces in paper, and places them in drawer.—Once rubs feces on leg like ointment.—Eats feces."*

Suddenly he feels something terrible grab him by the throat and drag him with it, into sleep, through sleep, beyond sleep. . . .

EIGHTEEN

16.IV.45

Arrived here yesterday after a dreadful journey—just to be bored out of my mind, it seems. There's nothing to read, and to kill the time have sent for some paper, on which I might as well make these notes.

The whole of Germany is smashed to pieces. Munich, Nuremberg, Dresden . . . all those magnificent towns look like glowing embers fresh from the stove. What is the point of it all? I had the Mercedes painted in camouflage colors, but once the driver and I still had to roll head over heels into a ditch, when an English fighter came at us with rattling machine guns. I didn't even have time to grab the dogs. Berlin is a sorry sight. Everywhere ruins, fire, and stench, windows boarded up, long lines outside the shops, even longer lines of bodies on the pavements, here and there a deserter strung up from a lamppost, old women being pushed along in baby carriages, people clambering over the smoldering ruins trying to find something of their family or their possessions. That wonderful city! It looks more like a natural disaster than the work of human beings, but perhaps it comes down to the same thing in the end. It will take more than a hundred years to put right. We picked our way through the chaos of fire engines and ambulances and people at their wits' end to the Chancellery, which had also taken a battering.

In the garden, at the dark entrance to the bunker, I was met by my brother-in-law Fegelein, who took me down an endless wrought-iron spiral staircase to the lowest floor, at least fifty steps underground. It seems that a few days ago the news of Roosevelt's death revived hope of a successful outcome; but I felt my arrival meant the beginning of the end—that I had come to die together with the Führer. But not just that. Before it is all over, I must and shall find out exactly what happened to Siggi, and why.

Adi was glad to see me but ordered me to return immediately to the mountain. When I refused, he seemed to be moved; he stared at me for a moment and left it at that. There was chocolate in the corner of his mouth, which I wiped away with my handkerchief.

17.IV.45

Did not manage to speak to him alone today either. In the last few months, he has aged years, his hair is almost completely gray, he has a stoop, the eyes in his sallow face are extinguished, his voice is broken, his left arm has a tremor, and he drags one leg. I can scarcely imagine that this is the same man that I knew just a few years ago—but no one can stand all those worries. He even has grease spots on his tie and his uniform; in the past that would have been unthinkable. All day long he is in meetings with his generals, at least if Dr. Morell is not filling him with injections and pills. My arrival marked the start of the great Russian offensive, as if I had a premonition. The bombing raids seem to be over; Goebbels says that the British and Americans are obviously leaving it to the Russians to finish the job. They themselves have swung southward in the direction of the Obersalzberg; they talk of the "alpine fortress" and appear to think that a

*huge army of ten thousand fanatical National Socialists is hidden
there, but that is nonsense; there is only a guard battalion. Meanwhile hundreds of thousands of Russkies are descending on us, like a
stream of lava from Vesuvius. Afterward there will be no more left of
Berlin than of Pompeii.*

*I had everything that was still usable in my suite in the Chan-
cellery brought down and have done my best to make my three stuffy
rooms as cheerful as possible, for Stasi and Negus, too. That is not
very easy, with all the concrete and no daylight, but it doesn't matter;
it can't last much longer. I'm perfectly happy to be so close to my poor
Adi. Everyone—Göring, Himmler, Ribbentrop, all of them—except
Goebbels—is trying to persuade him to leave Berlin while it is still
possible, to continue the fight at the Obersalzberg, or if need be escape
to the Middle East; but they don't know him. As far as he is concerned, everyone can go, but he is staying here. He is still the only one
who stands firm and thinks of his place in history.*

*In the afternoon went with Speer to the last concert of the Berlin
Philharmonic. I wore my beautiful silver-fox coat, probably for the
last time. Far away in the east, one could already hear the faint rum-
ble of the approaching front. In the car he said that he had replaced
the opening piece, Beethoven's* Egmont *Overture, with the finale of
Wagner's* Twilight of the Gods, *the burning Valhalla in which the
gods die. He also told me that he had had the files of the musicians
removed from the recruiting offices of the Home Guard. Goebbels
thought that they should go under, too. Since posterity had no right to
that brilliant orchestra. And if the Führer found out? I asked. I
should remind him, he said without looking at me, that in the past he
had used the same ruse to exempt artists with whom he was friendly
from military service. Speer is the only one who is not frightened of
the Chief like everyone else, and the Chief has no answer to that. A
little while ago, Adi seems to have issued his so-called Nero order, of*

scorched earth: everything necessary for the survival of the German people must be destroyed—all industries, harbors, railways, food supplies, population registers—everything necessary to live on even under the most primitive conditions, since it had proved inferior to the people from the east and hence forfeited its right to exist. I hear from the secretaries that Speer afterward traveled all around Germany countermanding the order and that he also told Hitler. Anyone else would have been shot immediately for even a fraction of such sabotage, but he was not even dismissed. It's a miracle. He is a hero and without doubt the best of the whole bunch, which makes the Chief's life a misery. I don't know, in some way they are in love with each other, those two—perhaps that is the bond that I have with Speer: we are a kind of trinity. Sometimes I think Adi loves him even more than me. I considered whether I should tell Speer: that I had recently had experience of administrative fraud myself, but then Siggi would have to be mentioned, and I didn't dare.

With our coats on, the lamps on the music stands as the only illumination, we listened to the music in the packed Beethoven Hall, while we knew that doom was approaching closer minute by minute. I had the impression that Speer was enjoying himself in that macabre situation; all through the concert, a superior smile played around his mouth. At the end Hitler Youth cadets stood at the exit distributing free cyanide capsules.

In bed thought for a long time of Siggi.

18.IV.45

Overwrought situation down here with increasingly desperate generals walking in and out who've lost their army and who pull themselves together completely when the Führer has promised them a new army, which of course does not even exist, although he would really only like to talk about food, his ailments, and the evil of the world in which everyone betrays him, except for Blondi and me. I have no idea what is really going on, and, to tell the truth, I couldn't care less; but meanwhile I'm even more bored than in the sanatorium. So to pass the days I'm going to write down what has happened to me in the last few months and what I know. No one will ever read it, because I shall dispose of it in good time. Just imagine if the Russians got hold of it.

That day in September, when I said good-bye to Siggi at the Berghof, I was not taken anywhere near Salzburg to fly to the Führer in the Wolf's Lair; we went in a completely different direction. When I asked the Gestapo man next to the driver the meaning of this, I was given no answer and realized that something ominous was going on. I was delivered to a kind of sanatorium in Bad Tölz behind high fences. It was clear to me that I must remain very calm now and not start shouting hysterically that I was the Führer's girlfriend and that I was the mother of his child, since that would only strengthen people in their conviction that I was mad. I was allowed to keep the dogs with me, so clearly people were after all aware that I wasn't just any patient. Of course I wanted to call Adi at once, but telephoning was forbidden.

In order to guard me, the Gestapo officer also remained in the institution; he had obviously been ordered not to exchange a word with me. Because I was confined to my room, he took Stasi and Negus for a walk a couple of times a day. The staff were very friendly, the food was fine, but no one told me anything. Even though I knew that Siggi was in good hands with Julia and Ullrich, I still worried about him. It was as though I were dreaming for the month I was imprisoned there. I looked at old fashion magazines or listened to the radio, which broadcast one depressing item of news after another. After just a few days, I gave up trying to find out what I had done wrong; the only thing I could think of was that for some reason I must now pay the price for the fact that I had found my way into the sinister regions of absolute power.

Then I was suddenly called to the phone in the office of the director, who left. Bormann on the line, and a little later the Chief's voice:

"Tschapperl! It's all been a misunderstanding! You'll be picked up this very afternoon and taken to the Berghof. But prepare yourself for some terrible news. There's been an accident. Siggi is dead."

It was as if the sun had suddenly risen and immediately afterward night had fallen. Looking back, I think I lost consciousness for a few seconds. As I was about to say something, he immediately interrupted me:

"Don't ask any more questions. It's terrible for me, too, but recently so many things have been terrible, and there are more to come. The world is a vale of tears. And remember not to behave at the Berghof like a mother who has lost her child."

A vale of tears, yes . . . but I could not cry. At the Berghof I was told about the so-called accident on the firing range, which I didn't believe a word of; there was a lot more behind it, because why had I been arrested myself? And that good-hearted Ullrich Falk, how could he have done that? Had he been paid? And had Julia accepted that? That was simply unthinkable! I couldn't ask them; in the meantime they had been transferred. Mittlstrasser maintained that he did not know where. The same afternoon I asked him if he would show me Siggi's grave, but in the cemetery of Berchtesgaden, his mouth fell open in astonishment. He pointed to the ground and said, "It was here, Miss Braun, right here, I'm sure of it. There was going to be a headstone." Was he pretending? Had there ever been a grave? Was Siggi still alive, and was he with Ullrich and Julia? No, I could see that his astonishment was genuine. We went to the administrator of the cemetery, but there was no Siegfried Falk to be found in his card index either. I said nothing. Of course they had dug him up and burned him. He must never have existed.

19.IV.45

Gradually I am beginning to despair of ever talking through the drama of our Siggi with Adi. How long have we left to live? A week? Two weeks? Perhaps that's precisely why there's no point, and perhaps he's avoiding it, but while we're still alive, we're not yet dead!

When Sergeant Major Tornow, Adolf's dog handler, went for a walk early this morning with Blondi and his own dachshund Schlumpi through the Tiergarten—that is, the bare expanse full of charred stumps that is left of it—I decided to join him with Stasi and Negus, even though Adi doesn't want me to go outside anymore. But he was still asleep; at most he would hear about it afterward from Rattenhuber, who is responsible for his personal security. At first Blondi was reluctant, not wanting to abandon her litter of puppies. Because of the smoke and stench and the dust of the dying city, it was scarcely a relief after the stale atmosphere of the bunker. I was struck by the blueness *of the light outside, after the dead, unmoving electric light down below. At the Brandenburg Gate, Hotel Adlon was on fire, but at last I could smoke a cigarette again. I had no need to be frightened, since no one knows me in Germany; one day that will be different. The pounding of the front had come closer still; it sounded like approaching thunder, or no, like the growling of a prehistoric beast crawling toward us destroying everything in its path. The excursion did not last long; grenades began to explode, and we had to retreat with the dogs.*

So now I'm fifteen yards underground again, and I must admit that I now feel more at home down here than outside. I'll go on from where I got to yesterday.

The evening of the same day, I phoned my parents and, despite the air-raid alarm, had myself driven to Munich. There I was finally put in the picture. They had been terrified when they had heard nothing from me for weeks and could not make contact with the Wolf's Lair. A few days after I had been taken to Bad Tölz, a Gestapo officer appeared and took my mother to headquarters. There she was told that she, Franziska Kronburger, had a Jewish grandmother and therefore was not 100 percent racially pure. That had emerged from the records of the Registry Office in Geiselhöring in Oberpfalz.

My parents were astounded, but I could not tell them what I immediately thought: that it was of course a plot, designed to discredit me and hence Siggi. So I was not racially pure, and neither was Siggi. But all they knew was that Siggi was the son of the Falks, who had died in a tragic accident. Meanwhile the Führer's son turned out to have Jewish blood! All hell had let loose! I know him, I know the rage he must have flown into when he received that news—

(The gremlins are here again: suddenly the light went out. I thought the end had come; the darkness was as complete as in a womb. I stayed sitting motionless with the pen in my hand and listened to the commotion in the corridor and in Adi's rooms next door. When Linge appeared with a pocket torch and a pack of candles, the light came back on.)

Adolf Hitler the father of a child contaminated with Jewish blood! That was the worst thing that could have possibly happened to him, and he did not hesitate for a moment in taking action. Gretl and her Fegelein now threatened to be caught up in the tragedy. Poor Gretl, she was three months pregnant—also with a non-pure-Aryan child. But was it all true? Mama came from a strict Catholic country family, and I myself had been educated by nuns at a convent school; we knew nothing about any Jews in the family. Papa tried desperately to reach the Chief, but of course he was unable to. Thank goodness he remembered one day that at his wedding he had had official copies made of his particulars and those of Mama, in case he ever needed them for a job application or something. He found them in the attic in an old shoe box, so that the forgery was crystal clear.

Only the Gestapo could be behind this. On whose orders? And why? Who had anything to fear from that little boy? But what makes me unhappiest of all is how Adi was capable of ordering the execution of his son, whom he adored. How on earth was it possible? I love him, but I don't understand him. Does he understand himself? Does he ever think about himself?

20.IV.45

Adi's birthday: fifty-six. Anyone who didn't know better would be more inclined to say seventy. Finally talked to him alone.

He got up at eleven, and a little later they all appeared to wish him a happy birthday—Bormann, Göring, Goebbels, Himmler, Ribbentrop, Speer, Keitel, Jodl, the whole club. They came via the tunnels from the bunkers under their own ministries and headquarters—not an unnecessary luxury, since the Americans had reappeared after all with a fleet of a thousand Flying Fortresses, which let their bombs rain down on the poor city for hours. Although we are under two yards of earth and five yards of concrete, on the lowest level there was constant pounding and cracking over our heads, the bunker shook, and here and there mortar dust fell. According to Goebbels it was intended as a birthday present, followed later in the day by a present from British bombers and a bombardment from the Russians, who can now reach the center of the city with their artillery. I cannot deny that I feel a little proud when I think that all those million-

strong armies and huge fleets of planes and those countless victims are needed to defeat the Chief. What woman has such a lover? He himself seems to find it all perfectly natural.

After the reception, despite the danger, he went up to the garden to present the Iron Cross to some members of the Hitler Youth drawn up on parade. I should have most liked to buttonhole Himmler to ask him if he knew anything about an operation by his Gestapo in the archives at Geiselhöring, but I didn't dare. The rest of the day was again devoted to discussions, and in the evening all the bigwigs scuttled off to safer parts. By tomorrow the encirclement of the city will probably be complete. I could see that they were frightened to death now that their own lives were at stake. All those cowards tried one last time to persuade the Chief to flee to Bavaria and conduct the war from there, but he is determined to die in Berlin. Speer also suddenly disappeared without saying good-bye; he is the only one I'm sorry I shall never see again. Of the intimates only Goebbels has stayed and, unfortunately, Bormann, too.

Later in the evening, with the four ladies of the secretariat and Miss Marzialy, the cook, we drank champagne in Hitler's small sitting room. He himself drank tea. In the exclusive company of women, he seemed to relax a little. As we had heard countless times previously, he spoke again of his political struggle in the 1920s, while eating biscuits nonstop, but now a few tears came into his eyes, because through the treachery and faithlessness of his generals, everything was lost. Nothing was spared him, he complained, and I saw that he was meanwhile checking his pulse. "And you?" he said to Blondi with her five suckling puppies. "Are you going to betray me, too?" Later he was again troubled by his periodic stomach cramps, for which Morell gives him medicines every day, and which in my view causes them. His secretaries Traudl and Christa pushed a chair under his legs and took the opportunity to wish him good night. A little later I was alone with him.

We looked at each other. He had biscuit crumbs in his mustache, and his breath smelled. In the past I would have done something that he needed me for; and I saw that he saw what I was thinking, because he always sees everything, but it was not spoken. That is over for good, like everything else.

"Our little Siggi is dead, Adi," I said. "Why?"

Under the portrait of his mother, and opposite the portrait of Frederick the Great, he glanced at me as if trying to remember who it could be, as if he first had to check through the countless people he had had executed in the meantime. Tenderly he stroked Wolfie, his favorite puppy, whom he had put on his lap with trembling hands.

"Because I got to hear that he was not racially pure."

"But that wasn't true."

"I didn't know that at the time."

"But he was Siggi, for God's sake!"

As he looked at me, his pale, waxy face became redder and redder, and suddenly he banged on the arm of his chair with a fist and yelled, "What do you think? That would have suited the Jews down to the ground! My son a Jewish bastard—a gift from heaven! I had had sexual relations with a non-Aryan! They would have laughed themselves silly. They actually said such things about me, as they did about Heydrich, but for some time past most of them haven't been laughing anymore."

"But be that as it may, he was still your own child!"

"Precisely. The admixture of Jewish blood had ruined my own proteins."

"But you could have simply let him stay Siegfried Falk, and no one would have been any the wiser."

"*And one day it would have come out. Someone would have talked about it. Falk, for instance. And if I had had him and Julia shot, someone would have talked whom they had talked to. In the end everything comes out. The world will be amazed at all the things that will come out shortly.*"

I was alarmed at the glow that suddenly lit up his eyes, and I was glad that I at any rate would never know.

"*And what would have happened to me if it had been true?*" *When he did not answer, I ventured cautiously,* "*Couldn't it be that the Gestapo—*"

"*Be quiet!*" *he interrupted me.* "*I cannot believe that my faithful Heinrich would do such a thing.*"

"*But who falsified those documents? And why?*"

"*I don't know. But perhaps I shall find out in the few days we have left.*"

Then he sent me away. He was tired. He suggested I have some more champagne with the secretaries.

21.IV.45

All day long the thunder of artillery bombardments, which no longer stop for a moment, and above us we can hear the proud Chancellery collapsing further and further, but you get used even to that. The worst thing for me is that I can no longer wash my clothes. I stink. Everyone who is left down here stinks. Adi, too.

22.IV.45

Morell has gone, too, thank God. At the invitation of the Führer, Goebbels and his family have moved into Morell's apartment. The little cripple is obviously delighted that he finally belongs to Hitler's innermost circle. They want to die with him. That is, Goebbels and his Magda want to—no one has asked their six small children. This afternoon I played with them and read to them from the "Max and Moritz" books. Helga, Holde, Hilde, Heide, Hedda, Helmut—in all those names there is an echo of "Hitler." Magda is determined to poison them, because a life without the Führer is no longer worth anything.

Adi was tied up all day in desperate discussions with Keitel and Jodl and other generals, while in the meantime he had raging telephone conversations with Dönitz and Himmler and heaven knows who else. In the evening I spoke to him briefly while he was sorting out his personal papers with a magnifying glass to have them burned in the garden. While it constantly creaked and pounded above our heads, I asked him what he thought of Magda's intention of murdering her children. Trembling, he held on to the edge of the table, looked straight at me for a few seconds, and said:

"That is her own free will; as far as I'm concerned, she can leave. But you should be glad Siggi is no longer alive. Otherwise you would have had to do the same with him in a little while. Or would you have preferred Stalin to put him on show in the Moscow Zoo?"

23.IV.45

It may be over any day, any hour now, but I don't care as long as I am with my love. Scarcely spoke to him today. Wrote farewell letter to Gretl, who is on the point of giving birth. Assured her—groundlessly—that she will definitely see Fegelein again.

Speer has suddenly reappeared in the citadel, and around midnight we drank a bottle of champagne in my room. He could not bear having left on Adi's birthday without saying good-bye. He called Hitler a "magnet." At the risk of life and limb, he flew through en-

emy fire in a small plane and landed on the Siegesallee near the Brandenburg Gate. He has no fear; in that he is definitely Adi's superior. I heard from him that this afternoon a telegram arrived from Göring in which he proposes taking over power when Hitler has ceased to be responsible for his actions. Bormann convinced the Führer that it was an attempted coup, whereupon Adolf relieved Göring of all his duties and issued an arrest warrant against him. But in reality, said Speer, it was more a coup by Bormann, eliminating his old rival from the succession to Hitler. With tears in his eyes, Adi seems to have shouted that now even his old comrade Göring had betrayed him and this was the end. I have no words to express how sorry I feel for him.

Tonight Speer left again. I hope he makes it.

24.IV.45

Today Adi suddenly appeared in my room and said without preamble, "Suppose it had been true and we had won the war and Siggi had become my successor—that would have been the ultimate coup by Jewry: Jewish blood would have had world domination and would have destroyed human civilization, because that is what the Jew, always and everywhere, is out for."

"The Jew, the Jew . . ." I repeated. "He would have been only one-eighth Jewish."

"An eighth!" he shouted contemptuously. "An eighth! Birdbrain! Why don't you read a book occasionally instead of just fashion magazines? Then you would know that every new generation throws up a full Jew according to Mendel's principles."

"But he wasn't even an eighth Jewish. He was a full-blooded Aryan." I gathered all my courage and said, "Someone deceived you, Adi."

When he turned around, he wobbled and had to hold on for support. Without another word he dragged himself out of the room. But I was left with a glad feeling: I was frightened that he had forgotten, because of all his concerns. However could I think that? He never forgets a thing.

Magda has to stay in bed. She has developed heart trouble at the prospect of having to poison her children. Yes, I count myself lucky that Siggi is no longer alive.

25.IV.45

I remember the enormous maps on the table in front of the window at the Berghof: Russia, Western Europe, the Balkans, North Africa. Now all that is lying on the map table is a map of Berlin. The Russians are already less than a mile away, in the Tiergarten, they are advancing toward us down every street and metro tunnel. A few more days and a plan of our bunker is all they'll need.

This afternoon ate lunch alone with him briefly, but I did not dare to bring up the subject of Siggi's execution again. Anyway, what's the point? As Adi downed his thin oat gruel, Linge brought the message that an armada of hundreds of heavy bombers had bombed the Obersalzberg, destroying everything, including the Berghof. It gave me a jolt: so now that part of my life had gone, too. But Adolf showed no emotion.

"Excellent," he said, nodding between mouthfuls. "Otherwise I would have had to do it myself."

26.IV.45

Problems with my brother-in-law. In the evening Hitler, Goebbels, Magda, and I were sitting together, the children were asleep, and the two men were talking about the moment when it had all gone wrong. I tried to cheer them up with memories of the parties we had had at the Berghof, but it was as if death were hanging in black curtains around the room. Suddenly I was called to the telephone by an orderly. I thought it might be my parents, but it was Fegelein. I asked where he was, but he did not answer. He said I must leave the Führer and immediately flee Berlin with him; in a few hours' time it would be too late. He was getting out, there was no point in dying an absurd death here for a hopeless cause, and I must not do that either. Horrified, I said that he should come straight back to the citadel, as the Führer knew no mercy with deserters. Then he hung up without saying good-bye. I said nothing about the conversation to Adi, but of course the line had been tapped, and he was told of it a little later. He gave orders that Fegelein should be tracked down and arrested.

Why did he phone me? Surely he knew they would listen in to the conversation. Was it perhaps a desperate effort to benefit from the official pass that I have? Poor Gretl. I just hope it turns out all right.

27.IV.45

I have not been outside for over a week, I know I shall never see the sun again, but I've resigned myself to that. I have lived for thirty-three years and got almost everything I longed for—why should I survive to the year 2000 as a woman of eighty-eight, in a bestial world left to run wild by the Bolsheviks? No, I am glad with all my heart that I can die here by my lover's side. In these days between life and death, I am often reminded of the first times I saw him, without knowing who he was. I was seventeen and had just started working as an assistant to Hoffmann, whom I was sometimes allowed to help in the darkroom. I liked it there in that mysterious red light, which gave me the feeling of being on another planet—and

I can still see his face looming up out of shiny nothingness in the developing tray like an apparition. Perhaps he enchanted me even then with those eyes of his.

Hermann arrested this afternoon. He was in his flat on the Bleibtreu-Strasse and was about to leave, in civilian clothes, with a bag full of money and precious items and accompanied by his mistress, the wife of an interned Hungarian diplomat, with whom he was going to flee to Switzerland. She was able to escape. Oh, how I hate that double traitor. I had the impression that Adi wanted him executed today, but with an appeal to Gretl's pregnancy, I managed to persuade the Chief just to demote and imprison him.

This afternoon Bormann asked me suspiciously whatever I was writing the whole time. He can't stand it if he doesn't know something, the brute. Farewell letters to my sisters and girlfriends, I said. Whenever I fill a sheet I hide it in the ventilation grill.

29.IV.45

I'm Mrs. Hitler! This is the most wonderful day of my life: Eva Hitler! Eva Hitler! Mrs. Eva Hitler-Braun, wife of the Führer! The first lady of Germany! I'm the happiest person in the world! At the same time, it is the last day of my life, but what could be more beautiful than to die on one's most wonderful day?

The time has come. Last night at ten o'clock, I heard Adi suddenly roar like a wild beast, as I had never heard before, but I did not dare go to his rooms. Goebbels told me an hour later that the Führer had been presented with an intercepted report from a British news agency, revealing that Himmler had begun peace negotiations with the West via the Swedish Count Bernadotte. Himmler! After Göring, his most faithful follower and last remaining candidate for the succession, had finally also betrayed him. This was the worst thing that

could have happened to him, said Goebbels, and it meant the end of
us all.

I had no idea of all the things that were happening in the citadel
in the next few hours. Meanwhile Sunday had come, no one slept,
most of us will never sleep again, and at one in the morning Adi was
suddenly standing in my room, almost unrecognizable, his hair disheveled, unshaven, his face full of red blotches. Shivering all over his
body, he flopped onto my bed and rubbed his face with both hands. After he had composed himself a little, he told me what I already knew,
and that he had given orders for Himmler to be arrested and shot.
Without saying anything, I sat down next to him on the floor and
took his beautiful, cold hand in mine. He looked at me and said, while
his eyes became moist, "It's all clear to me now, Tschapperl. Fifteen
years ago, even before the takeover of power, I had an investigation
carried out to check whether you and your family were pure Aryan.
Perhaps you can appreciate that I could not take any chances in
that respect. For some reason I had it done by Bormann and not
by Himmler, who had already opened dossiers on everything and
everyone—on you of course, and even on me, I suspect. Today I think
that my intuition, which has never yet deceived me, was giving me
the first signal that he was not 100 percent trustworthy. That investigation came up with nothing, and so for me the matter was closed.
But not for Himmler. He felt passed over, which he had been, and
from then on he waited for the moment when he could get even. Do
you remember," he suddenly asked, "that we were once sitting together on the terrace at the Berghof—you, Bormann, and I—and I
said that I might found a dynasty, like Julius Caesar?"

"Vaguely."

"But I remember as if it were yesterday. Julia was just putting
coffee and cakes on the table—and I deliberately said it while she was

there, so that she could get used to the fact that one day she might have to relinquish Siggi. At the time I was toying with the idea of marrying you after the final victory. That was to be the most dazzling wedding of all time here in Germania, with weeks of festivities in the whole Pan-German World Empire. On his twenty-first birthday, in 1959, Siegfried Hitler would succeed me as Augustus to my Caesar. You and I would retire to Linz, where I, as an old man of seventy, would devote myself exclusively to art and supervise with Speer the construction of my mausoleum on the Danube, that was to be many times larger than that of Napoleon's in the Dôme des Invalides."

A powerful direct hit just above our heads made the bunker shake in the soft earth. Adi flinched and looked anxiously at a stream of mortar dust trickling down in the corner of the room.

"That's all over now," I said.

"Through treachery, incompetence, and lack of fanaticism." He nodded. "Of course I should never have said that at the time, because you must never say anything if it is not strictly necessary, but I said it, and Bormann passed it on to his friend Fegelein, when he was half drunk, of course. He in turn should not have done that, but he did, and Fegelein passed it on to Himmler, whose liaison officer he was. Of course Himmler had known for a long time that we had a son; otherwise he would have been no good as a policeman. And then," said Adi, "last summer, when everything was starting to go wrong and those treacherous swine tried to assassinate me, your brother-in-law went to Himmler and said he wanted to be rid of your pregnant sister. Divorce was naturally out of the question, because that marriage had been my wish, and I had even acted as a witness. And my treacherous chief of police had the answer. He had the papers in Geiselhöring falsified, so killing three birds with one stone: Fegelein would *have his way, but what he was really after was that Siggi would not survive, because Siggi stood in the way of his aspirations to succeed me. And incidentally that old score with Bormann was settled."*

Whatever possessed those men? I did not know what to say and asked, "How do you know all this?"

"From Fegelein. When I heard about Himmler's treachery I suspected at once that the aim of his intended flight to Switzerland was to make contact from there with the Allies, and I immediately had him grilled."

"What will happen to him now?"

He looked at me, and for a moment his eyes turned into two knives, or axes—I don't know how to express it.

"It's already happened."

I looked down and thought of Gretl's child, who would never know its father.

"At the time," Adi went on a little later, "I gave Bormann a dressing-down for having bungled things in 1930. I sent him to the Obersalzberg to order Falk to eliminate Siggi, and I think he already suspected that things did not add up but did not dare tell me, even after your father had shown that the documents had been falsified. Or perhaps he did not want to say because he also had the dream of succeeding me. But I shan't ask him all that, because it no longer matters. I will have no successor; I was an idiot to think that National Socialism would survive me. And for a thousand years at that. Everyone has always underestimated me, but myself most of all. It began with me, and it will end with me. Dönitz can clear up the rubble, as far as I'm concerned; it leaves me cold. Instead of thinking about my successor, I have made another decision, Tschapperl. To make it up to you, I'm going to marry you right away."

Had I heard correctly? Was Adolf Hitler going to marry me? Surely that couldn't be true? I had been waiting for those words all my life! My heart leaped. I sat up with a jerk and, crying with happiness, embraced him. While I was kissing him, there was a knock, and I stood up in alarm, as I had done for all those years—but it wasn't really necessary anymore: in a little while the whole world would finally know who I was! Linge reported that Colonel General Ritter von Greim was awaiting instructions, whereupon my fiancé, helped by the two of us, stood up with a groan.

While I quickly combed his hair, he said, "Everyone will wonder for centuries why I'm doing this, but only you will know."

I immediately went to get changed. I should have most liked to get married in white, but I haven't anything of the kind here in my wardrobe; instead I put on Adi's favorite black silk dress with the roses, and with it the loveliest jewelry I had been given by him: the gold bracelet with the tourmalines, my watch with brilliants, the topaz necklace, and the brilliant hairpin. I still have them all on—and I know that I shall never take them off.

Goebbels had meanwhile had an official located with powers to solemnize our marriage.

"His name is Wagner," said Goebbels with shining eyes as I went to the map room on his arm at two in the morning. "What do you say to that? Wagner—here in this Twilight of the Gods! The Führer still has magical power over reality."

He and a surly-looking Bormann were our witnesses. Apart from that there were a few generals; Magda, constantly casting jealous looks at me; the ladies from the secretariat; and Constanze Marzialy, who will shortly cook our farewell meal: spaghetti with tomato sauce. Wagner was in the uniform of the Home Guard, and when I had to confirm that I was of pure Aryan descent, I realized that Adi had wanted to hear that "Yes" from my own mouth. But he cannot have been as happy as when I heard his "Yes" in reply to the question of whether he took me as his lawful, wedded wife—those three letters, *that short sound, which for me meant heaven on earth. When I signed the certificate after him on the map table, by the trembling index finger of Wagner, I saw that a large cross had been drawn in red pencil across the map of Berlin. This is the last thing that I shall write. There is already street fighting in the Wilhelmstrasse; the Russians may appear in the bunker at any time. My husband has dictated his will and on top of everything had to endure the report of Mussolini's end: shot by partisans and hung upside down from a gasoline pump with his girlfriend, Clara Petacci. "Just like St. Peter," said Goebbels with the cynical humor on which he has the patent. That is exactly what must not happen to us, and my husband has had gasoline delivered to burn our bodies in a little while.*

In the corridor Magda's children are running about making a terrible din, but no one says anything, for their fate is also sealed. I am reminded of Siggi but try to suppress the thought that I owe my happiness to his death.

Half an hour ago my husband had Blondi poisoned by Tornow. He no longer trusted the cyanide capsules that he had been given by Himmler and which are intended for me. She died immediately; silently, without emotion, he looked at his favorite animal for a moment and turned away. Ten minutes ago Tornow suddenly appeared in my room, with his Schlumpi under his arm, who started wagging his tail when he saw me. With tears in his eyes, he said that he had had to take Blondi into the garden and on my husband's orders had to shoot her five puppies, including little Wolfie, as they hunted for the teats of their dead mother. I did not understand what he had come for, whereupon he stared silently at Stasi and Negus, who were sitting next to each other on the bed.

"It's not true!" I cried. "Surely the Russians can have them!" I went numb and looked at his dachshund, a chocolate-colored sweetie with a brown nose. He started crying and without a word disap-

peared with the three dogs. Fortunately I cannot hear the shots. When he comes back, I shall ask him to burn this manuscript in the garden. He is the only one I can trust here.

I can't go on. I don't know what to do. I love my husband, but what possesses him? Nine dogs! Why? In a little while he'll knock politely on the door to fetch me for our wedding night in the flames.

NINETEEN

When Maria returned to the room, she froze on the threshold. She saw immediately that something fateful had happened. Herter was still lying in the same position in which she had left him, with eyes closed, but at the same time he had altered beyond recognition, as if he had been exchanged for his image from the waxworks in Amsterdam.

"Rudi!" she screamed.

Without closing the door behind her, she ran to the bed and shook him to and fro by his shoulders. When he did not react, she listened at his mouth. Silence. With trembling fingers she loosened his tie, tried to unbutton his shirt, then tore the sides apart and laid her ear to his chest. Deep silence everywhere. As well as she could, she tried mouth-to-mouth resuscitation, heart massage, but to no effect. At her wits' end, heart pounding, she sat up and looked at his unreal face.

"I don't believe it!" she cried. She grabbed the telephone and phoned reception. "Send a doctor at once! At once!" Sobbing, she embraced the lifeless body that seemed to want nothing more to do with her, while keeping at bay with all her might the idea that he might be dead.

The doctor, a small man with curly black hair, was in the room a few moments later. Without saying anything, all his attention on the motionless body, he sat down on the edge of the bed and lifted Herter's left hand in order to take his pulse. Something shiny fell from the hand onto the floor. He picked it up, studied it for a moment, and gave it to Maria. In astonishment she looked at the weirdly shaped piece of metal, lead perhaps, which she had never seen. What kind of mysterious thing was it? Where did it come from? Why had he picked it up?

The examination with the stethoscope produced no expression on the doctor's face that gave hope. Carefully he moved Herter's eyelids apart and shone a flashlight into his pupil.

He sighed, looked at Maria, and said, "I'm sorry, madam. The gentleman is dead."

"But how can it have happened so suddenly?" asked Maria, as if an answer to that question could still turn things around. "He was alive half an hour ago!"

The doctor got up. "His heart suddenly stopped. That's possible at this age. Perhaps through an excess of emotion."

"But he was just going to have a nap!"

The doctor made a gesture indicating that he was equally mystified; he took his leave with a few more words of sympathy. The manager of the Sacher had meanwhile appeared in the room. Very upset, he took Maria's hands in his and tried to find words.

"Madam . . . such a great mind . . . a loss to the world . . ." he blurted out. "Of course we shall help you with everything."

Maria nodded. "I'd like to be alone with him now for a little while."

"Of course, of course," said the manager, and he left the room, shutting the door gently behind him.

Maria felt the irrevocable fact starting to sink in. What was to become of her she could deal with later; now she must call Olga at once. Poor little Marnix! How were they to tell him?

In Amsterdam there was no answer, and she got the voice mail.

"It's Maria," she said after the tone. "Dear Olga, something terrible has happened. Prepare yourself for the worst. Rudi suddenly died just now. In his sleep . . ." She felt something like paralysis, but she forced herself to go on talking. "Phone back to the Sacher right away. You've got the number. I hope you come home before you go to Schiphol; otherwise I'll try to reach you there. Perhaps it'll be better if Marnix hears from me that—" Her voice broke. "I can't speak anymore. . . ." she said hoarsely and put the receiver down.

With the shiny piece of metal in her hands, she looked at Herter, her face wet with tears. "Where have you gone to?" she whispered.

Her gaze fell on the cassette recorder in Herter's right hand. While her eyes widened a little, she got up and tried to take it out, but the fingers held on to it. She carefully extricated it, feeling that the body had already grown colder.

The tape had stopped at the end. In the chair by the window, she rewound it, listening to it briefly now and again.

Suddenly she heard, ". . . The bodies were laid in a grenade crater close to the exit and quickly had gasoline poured over them. Because no one dared venture into the ring of fire again, Adjutant Linge threw a burning cloth on top—and a policeman who saw the scene from a distance testified later that it was as if the flames flared up from their bodies of their own accord.

Of their own accord! So that was Nietzsche's torch! . . . I can't keep my eyes open any longer. . . ." Then her own voice: "I can imagine. Go and sleep for a bit; you've got half an hour or so. The embassy car will be here in an hour. I'll go downstairs and have a Viennese coffee—to bring me around. If you need me, just ring."

She heard the door of the room close, after which there was silence. She remained listening intently. For minute after minute, there was nothing to be heard, just the traffic outside in the street. When the telephone rang, she turned the machine off.

"Olga?"

"No, madam, the driver from the embassy. I'm down in the lobby ready to take you and Mr. Herter to the airport. Mrs. Röell sends her apologies—she gave birth to a girl this afternoon."

"No, there's been a terrible accident, driver. Mr. Herter is dead. Please ask the ambassador to call me as soon as possible."

When the driver was obviously too taken aback to answer, she hung up.

She turned the recorder on again and went on listening to the silence, not taking her eyes off Herter's face. Outside there was the clip-clop of horses' hooves. After a few minutes, she suddenly heard a faint hubbub that she could not place—and then, very faint and distant, his voice. Groaning, sounds, words . . . She covered up one ear and closed her eyes with effort. Not until she had played it for the third time did she understand:

". . . *he* . . . *he* . . . *he* is here . . ."

Then nothing more.